AMRO 35~

1989

Books by Samuel Hazo

FICTION
Stills
The Wanton Summer Air
The Very Fall of the Sun
Inscripts

POETRY
Silence Spoken Here
Nightwords
The Color of Reluctance
Thank a Bored Angel
To Paris
Quartered
Once for the Last Bandit
Twelve Poems
Blood Rights
My Sons in God
Listen with the Eye
The Quiet Wars
Discovery

TRANSLATIONS
Transformations of the Lover
The Growl of Deeper Waters
The Blood of Adonis

CRITICISM
Smithereened Apart: A Critique of Hart Crane

ESSAYS
The Pittsburgh that Starts Within You
The Feast of Icarus

STILLS

STILLS

SAMUEL HAZO

Atheneum

NEW YORK

1989

This is a work of fiction. Any references to
historical events; to real people, living or
dead; or to real locales are intended only to
give the fiction a setting in historical reality.
Other names, characters, and incidents either are the product of the author's imagination or are used fictitiously, and their resemblance, if any, to real-life counterparts is
entirely coincidental.

Atheneum
Macmillan Publishing Company
866 Third Avenue, New York,
N.Y. 10022

Collier Macmillan Canada, Inc.

Library of Congress Cataloging-in-Publication Data
Hazo, Samuel John.
Stills / Samuel Hazo.
p. cm.
ISBN 0-689-12058-3
I. Title
PS3515.A9877S75 1989
813'.54—dc19 89-17 CIP

10 9 8 7 6 5 4 3 2 1

Printed in the United States of America

For
MARGARET
TALCOTT

STILLS

HE WHITENESS OF THE TWA TERMINAL will be whiter against the slush-gray sky. From horizon to horizon the weighty clouds will roll and tumble south by southeast. They will shift and change shapes like bellows of smoke from a battery of stacks beyond Long Island Sound. The rain that falls will be finer than spindrift.

Departing and arriving aircraft will await their turn on the runways. On the international side a Lufthansa 747 will trundle into position for taxiing, and the seven jets positioned behind it will ease forward like elephants, nose-to-tail, and stop. The vapor of their muted jet spoors will shimmer in the slowly descending darkness.

Like an overweight runner breaking from his starting blocks, the Lufthansa jumbo jet will lumber slowly down the tarmac. As it accelerates, it will appear to grow lighter and more buoyant within the fury of its own power and, filling the dusk with the blending whines of its jets, it will rise and aim the flying cross of itself steeply into the slushy sky. Moments later a Lear jet will vector to land on the same runway. Descending by degrees, it will dawdle in the updrafts and downdrafts, but it will keep to its pattern until its twin wheels straddle the spine of the runway. With its tail wheel still suspended, it will streak past the waiting jets—a white gull vivid against the herd.

A man in a belted black raincoat will watch the flights from the TWA lounge. He will be necklaced with two cameras. The lenses of both cameras will be uncapped. The black finish of one of the cameras, a Nikon, will be worn off at the edges of the case and the lens rims so that the basic metal will show through, and its sister camera, a Hasselblad, will have similar gray weatherings. The man himself will bear a strong resemblance to Charles Lindbergh, young in the eyes but lean in the cheeks. His uncombed brown hair will have some gray in it, dominant at the sideburns and interspersed elsewhere. He will watch the departing and incoming flights for several minutes and then sit in one of the padded chairs. He will pick up an abandoned copy of the *New York Times,* start to read it, then frown and put it back on the coffee table where he found it. Returning to the window that overlooks the far runways, he will watch the jets like a sailor sizing up the sea.

THE WOMAN IS NIBBLING THE ERASER END of a yellow pencil. A notebook is splayed on her lap, but there is nothing on the open pages except a spiral of circles slendering tornado-like from top to bottom on the left and the start of another smaller tornado on the right. The woman is seated on a swivel chair. She is listening to something—a record, a tape, the silence, something. In front of her is an old railroader's desk with the cover rolled up halfway, and the top of the desk is strewn with newspaper clippings, magazines, several books and stacks of black-and-white photographs of various sizes. Behind the woman is a bookcase made of brick supports and shelves of unfinished white pine boards. Books fill the shelves every which way.

It is obvious that the woman does not rhyme with these surroundings. Everything about her conveys a sense of neatness while everything in the room is in some state of intentional disarray. The untidiness does not bother her. She continues to nibble on the pencil's eraser like a student trying to think of an answer during a difficult examination. Her eyes give the impression of having an intelligence of their own. The firm set of her jaw suggests that she is used to making decisions and that she is about to make another one if she can only define the problem. Her hair is parted in the middle and combed on both sides of the part straight back over her ears to the nape of her neck, and the hairs seem permanently trained in that orientation. In profile she resembles a diver emerging from a pool, the hair sleeked down and back, the cheeks lean, the chin taut. From the front her face is fuller than the profile suggests, and the straight, Greco-Roman nose seems almost plain. Her left eyebrow is a fraction more arched than her right, so that even in a moment of complete composure she looks as if she is about to ask a question.

Whatever the woman is listening to or for suddenly makes her frown. She reaches to her right and depresses the forward button of a compact tape recorder with the same care that a typist would exercise to make a correction on an otherwise flawless page. Then she leans back in the swivel chair and listens again to the voice she was listening to before reversing the tape to its beginning. It is a man's voice with an edge of tiredness and cynicism to it that is as much a part of it as its pitch.

". . . three, two, one. Just testing now to see if this thing is picking me up. It's October 7, 1985, Tom, so you know when I made this tape. It's Lebanon tomorrow or the day or so after tomorrow. There's a way to get into the country through Cyprus. You can pick up a ferry there and make the crossing to a port above Beirut. The only other way is the airport, and that's dicey. I'll see if I can get some good shots there. Black-and-white, of course. Can't improve on that. My camera is a good, old tool to me, Tom. I'm comfortable just holding it. I said that to a priest once in Spain, just east of Barcelona. I know you're a Catholic, Tom, so you would have understood the reference. At the time I didn't know what he was talking about when he said he felt the same way when he held his breviary in his hand. Mercedes explained it to me years later, and I understood that the priest and I were both talking the same language. We were both talking about something that gave us security, don't you see?

"How old are you now, Tom? I'm guessing that you're about five years younger than I am, and I'm just forty-eight. At least I think I'm forty-eight. Since Mercedes died, I don't worry about the count. Sorry. The only thing I want to do right now is to make this tape for you before I leave. I just want to have my say about a few particulars to clear my mind, and there's no one I'd rather say them to than you. You and I always got along. Better than brothers, really. Without Mercedes I just keep everything to myself, and that's not good. But what's the alternative? You can't create a mate. And there will never be another woman like your sister, Tom. Mercedes was the best, the best for me. I'm lost without her.

"Did you and Mercedes share things, Tom? I suppose it was the same for a brother and sister as it was for my brother and me. When he and I were growing up, we used to talk a lot. Good talks. Nothing phony. He'd be about your age now if it hadn't been for Vietnam. No, he would have been a year younger. A land mine got him north of Saigon. A lot of them died that way over there. It either killed them outright or blew their legs off or blew what they had between their legs off. My photo of those seven men in wheelchairs at the VA Hospital is the ultimate photo of that damned war. There they were on their stumps, waiting, just waiting. The wheelchair business never had it so good as it did after that war.

"Lyndon's war. LBJ. They tried to slap initials on Kennedy, remember? JFK. Like an echo of FDR. It never really took. He was always Jack Kennedy. But LBJ was perfect for Johnson. Like initials on a branding iron. He branded his wife and his daughters with it. And the ranch. LBJ was on everything. Think about it. Some ego. Bigger than south Texas. I lay the war at his doorstep. It was a lousy war to cover. Of course, there were some good photographers in Vietnam. None of them was like me or Capa or Mydans or Margaret. Margaret Bourke-White, I mean. But there were some good ones. The photo of the naked little girl running in panic down the street away from the napalm toward the photographer is a great photo. The fear in her eyes and in her body comes right off the paper at you. You have to turn your eyes away from it. At least I do. Then there was the other one of the prisoner being shot from three inches away by that Saigon colonel or whatever he was. But on second thought I don't think either of those photos was really a photograph. They were prints from a film. Most of the camera work there was with sixteen-millimeter. Just point the camera and let her roll. You had to come away with something.

"It's different when you're working with stills. One shot at a time. You have to be ready or lucky at just the right instant. Half skill, half luck, all instinct. But if you are lucky and know what to do with a camera at the right moment, you can come away with something that is really something. Like Cartier-Bresson's stuff at his best—the one of the two Greek peasant women marching like soldiers under the caryatids or the one of the French boy bringing home the dinner wine like the man of the house or that other one of the Mexican whores with the whore-makeup and the whore-eyes as they look for business through the shack window. Like Capa's great photograph of the Spanish militiaman getting hit just at the moment of the hit. You can learn a lot about modern war just by studying that photograph, Tom—a soldier being killed by a bullet from a rifle in someone's hands a half-mile away. The anonymous, impersonal bullet. And from there you jump to the anonymous, impersonal bomb. The executioners never see the ones they're executing. Death at a respectable distance. Clean.

"One thing I want to bring back from Lebanon is the face of horror at close quarters. I want to take a photo that will last. Like Capa's. I keep it here in the house. I look at it every day. It's like a poem. I see something more in it every time I look at it. I'll show it to you whenever I get back,

Tom. And while I'm thinking about it, I want to thank you for the cigars. I'm smoking one of them right now while I'm talking into this gizmo. I puff on it every time I take a pause, and that gives me a chance to think, and then I go on. That's what Mark Twain asked for the day before he died—did you know that? A cigar. No, I take it back. It wasn't a cigar. It was tobacco. Tobacco for his pipe. And so he had one good smoke the day before he died, and he must have enjoyed the hell out of it. And what difference did it make? He died the next day anyway, and that was probably the day he was scheduled to die in the first place, and at least he had one good pipeful on the way. I feel like talking tonight, Tom, so you might as well bear with me. If I sound a little fatalistic, that's just the way I've gotten since . . . You don't have to listen to all this straight through. Just turn it off whenever you want, and then come back to it. Or else throw it out. The tape's yours, so you can do what you want with it . . ."

The telephone on the railroader's desk rings. Stopping the tape recorder with a press on the pause button, the woman reaches for the telephone after the second ring. She appears annoyed by the interruption, but the annoyance is reflected in her eyes only, not in the tone of her voice when she speaks.

"Hello."

"It's Tom, Louise. How's it going?"

"I've been sorting through a lot of papers and magazines and photographs most of the morning. Now I'm listening to the tape you lent to me."

"You have over an hour of listening ahead of you."

"I'm not sure I should be listening to this, Tom. It seems

too personal. It was something left for your ears. Alone. I feel like an eavesdropper."

"You're not an eavesdropper unless you're listening when you shouldn't be. This is different. One of the things that Bax says on that tape is that I can do what I want with it. Now that he's gone, I'm taking his advice. I want you to listen to it, Louise. It's all there is. Bax never wrote letters. At least he never wrote letters to me. My sister used to keep me up to date when they were out of the country, but Bax didn't believe in writing. It wasn't his medium." He pauses. "Are you still there?"

"Sorry. I was just thinking. He talks into a tape recorder the way I do sometimes. I just let myself go, let the thoughts come out, and then I listen to it afterward. It's amazing what you can learn about yourself that way, Tom. It's like looking into a mirror. You get good at picking out the defects."

"Well, maybe the tape recorder was his medium. His second medium."

"There's no question that the camera was the first. I've been looking through his photographs—the ones in his book, and then there are stacks and stacks of black-and-white glossies. And there are a lot that are dry-mounted. They're remarkable." She pauses. "Tell me something, Tom. Why did he use the name of Diogenes when he signed his photos?"

"That was his middle name. His real middle name."

"You've got to be kidding."

"No, I'm not. His father was a Latin teacher or a Greek teacher, one of the two. Bax told me it embarrassed him when he was a kid to have a middle name like that. For a long while he was just Bede D. Baxter. Try to say that fast,

9
•

and you'll see why it didn't work for him. Then he was just
Bede Baxter. He signed his early work that way. But then
he decided that Bede Baxter sounded like one of those
Hollywood fake names that actors adopted in the thirties
and forties. So he read up on Diogenes. He told me there
was one story about Diogenes watching a mouse. The
mouse just kept following his nose to the cheese. Diogenes
saw himself as a kind of philosophical mouse, following his
mind wherever it led him. Bax saw parallels between that
and his work as a photographer, so he started to use Diogenes as his professional name."

While Tom has been talking to her, Louise has been
sorting through a stack of photographs on the desk. She
turns the top photograph toward her so that the shine of the
light does not distort it. It's a picture of a narrow street in
France, Italy, Algeria, Morocco? She can't be sure. The bed
of the street is cobbled, and the cobblestones glisten with
new rain. On either side of the street are balconies, and the
balcony windows are all shuttered. Seated on a doorstep in
the right hand corner of the photograph is a boy of no more
than seven or eight. He is looking directly at the photographer. The expression on the boy's face is not one of suspicion or dislike or even of curiosity. It is the look of obedience, of trust. Total trust. The more that Louise looks at the
photograph, the more the look of obedience or trust begins
to dominate, even define the photograph. She feels that she
will remember the boy's expression for the rest of her life.
She turns over the photograph and reads: "I can't forget the
look on this boy's face—Bax." Shocked by the exact corrob-
oration of her feeling by Bax's words scrawled in grease
pencil on the reverse side of the photograph, she momentarily forgets that she is listening to Tom.

"Are you still there, Louise?"

"Yes, Tom. I was just looking at something here. I'm sorry. What were you saying?"

"I was about to say that your husband called. I mean your ex-husband called."

"Harry?"

"Yes."

"Did he say what he wanted?"

"He said he'd get in touch with you tomorrow. He said very urgently that it wasn't really urgent. I didn't think you wanted me to give him the telephone number where you are. Or maybe you did?"

"No. I'm glad you didn't. But you certainly pinpointed Harry's style. He always made everything seem urgent. That was his problem." She laughs, but there is really no laughter in the laugh. She shifts the receiver to her left ear. "I think I'm going to spend the rest of the evening here, Tom. You know, it's absolutely amazing how you can get to know a person through his work, and the fact that I'm in his home is a real plus. He was a very interesting man, your brother-in-law."

"Interesting and talented. He won every award that exists in photography. And that's the reason I asked you to take on this job. I want a program that will really commemorate him. Not just another memorial. You're familiar with those, I know."

"Quite familiar."

"Louise, you're the only one on the whole staff here who has the sensitivity to know what I want."

"Thanks, Tom. I hope I don't let you down."

"Is there anything you need?"

"No. So far I've confined myself to the study and the

workshop here. Later I might take a tour of the house if it's all right with you."

"Feel free."

"It looks as if everything is just the way he left it."

"Well, not exactly. I was there once or twice over the past few months. I straightened up a little. I didn't stay very long. It was, well . . ."

"It was hard for you."

"Yes." Tom waits and then says, "Have you eaten anything?"

"About an hour ago I took a break. I found some coffee in the kitchen, so I perked a few cups for myself. Black. I couldn't find the sugar anywhere. But I did find some cheese and crackers in the refrigerator. The cheese was still good. Swiss."

"After five months?"

"It was still good Swiss, Tom."

"Well, call me if you need anything. I'll be working late tonight."

"I'll stay here until I get too tired to listen. If Harry calls for me again, tell him I'll call him back tomorrow. Good night, Tom."

"Take care, Louise."

Louise turns the tape recorder on again and swivels the chair so that she is facing two large photographs mounted on the opposite wall. One photograph is of a group of spectators in a section of an end zone in a football stadium. They are cheering and smiling as if cheering and smiling are the answer to everything they've ever wanted. They also look as if they are overjoyed at being photographed. The second photograph is of three spectators at the scene of a traffic accident. One of the spectators is looking down at the body of a man facedown on the road beside an overturned panel truck. The other two spectators are facing the camera and smiling broadly. Their smiles and the smiles of the spectators in the end zone in the first photograph are exactly the same.

". . . only time I forgot to take a picture was when I got involved in a childbirth. It happened about three years before I met you and Mercedes. I was in Algeria to take some follow-up pictures after the war. I was in the interior, and I got sidetracked with a little girl and her mother as I was leaving one of the villages. The woman was pregnant and then some, and the little girl was holding her hand. We walked along more or less as a group for a while, and then the woman started to moan. When I turned, I saw her sitting and then sprawling on the side of the road. The little girl looked scared to death, and the woman was sweating and screaming softly every few seconds. I knew I should be helping, but the photographer in me took over. The girl kept looking at me, asking me with her eyes to do something, and the woman was holding the girl's hand as if it were the last hand in the world. I kept thinking that this would make a great picture, so I got the camera ready. I started walking back, and then the woman screamed, and the baby slid out from under her skirt just like that, slick as grease. I never saw anything happen so fast. I didn't even have time to focus. Then after just a few minutes the woman picked up the baby and bit the cord with her side teeth and tied what was left of it in a little knot and limped off with the little girl behind her.

"Later, when I told the story to Mercedes, she asked me

why I didn't help the woman. She always looked at the human side of events, Tom. She said that professionalism only went so far. In a human crisis of any kind, she said you had the duty to be human, nothing less, nothing more. I told her that photographers couldn't think that way. If they did, there would be no great photographs. A photographer has to distance himself from what's happening so he can frame the event. He has to become a lens. He has to let depth of field really become depth of field. He has to find the range, not too close, not too far. But Mercedes would just shake her head. She told me once that there was nothing more important than life itself. Everything else for her had value only in relation to that, whether I thought it was subject matter for a photograph or not. The only answer I could ever give her was to say that at the crucial moment you have to decide if you're a photographer or part of what's happening. You can't have it both ways.

"Too bad we never had children, Tom. Mercedes loved children. She was always grateful that she was the aunt to your three, you know that. We wanted children. It just didn't happen. Some people have children as easy as you please. Not us. Mercedes was never envious of other women who had children, but still it hurt her to know that we didn't have one of our own.

"Tom, I have to tell you, man-to-man, that these past couple of years have been tough, the toughest I've ever lived through in my life. It takes everything I have to concentrate on my work. I dream up projects for myself, and for a while it's a challenge, and then I just get tired of them. I travel to see if a change of scene will pick me up. It works for a couple of days, maybe a week, but after that I have

myself on my hands. And the hardest thing is to come back
to the house. As soon as I unlock the door and walk in, the
past just hits me in the face, and I'm no further ahead than
when I left. All this sounds like I'm crying on your shoulder, I know. But I'm down to my last cards now. The things
that used to interest me don't interest me anymore. You
remember how we would talk politics, you and I? It's like
another world to me now. I used to think in the Kennedy
days that the country was starting to find itself again. Of
course, all the reconstructionists are having a hard look at
Kennedy now, and some of the shine has come off the
apple, but there was something in the air when he was alive
that died with him. And there was real grief in the hearts
of a lot of people when he was killed. Not just in the United
States but all over the world. It wasn't faked. It was real. So
there was something in the man that got across to people.

"I haven't recognized the country since. I feel like an
alien, honest to God. First there was Johnson. Then we got
Nixon. He won every state but one the second time around,
and then he was out on his ass. But he's still at large, still
Nixon. And people are listening to him like he's president
for life. It's unbelievable to me. And then there was Ford.
And Carter. Middleweights, both of them. And now we
have Reagan.

"I photographed all of them, Tom. Kennedy actually
looked older close up, and younger far away. Johnson always reminded me of a foreman on some field job in Texas.
Nixon had the same pudgy look I saw when I photographed
Batista. Grumpy, and his eyes never stayed on you very
long. The same with Batista. He's living like a pasha somewhere in Spain. Up close he looks like a fat sergeant who

won the sweepstakes. Once a sergeant, always a sergeant. Later I photographed Ford in Michigan, and then Carter on his farm in Georgia.

"If you study the faces, Tom, you almost get a feel for the country. Not one of them stops you in your tracks. Like Lincoln's, for example. Or Teddy Roosevelt's. Or Wilson's. Or FDR's. And I'm not one of the millions who think Reagan is the answer to everything. Everything about his style is unreal to me. I try to find out what he stands for, and it comes down to Christ and capitalism. That's it.

"I feel out of step these days. We have a habit of backing the wrong countries all over the world, or the wrong people in the right countries. I saw that at close quarters in Lebanon, Tom. We got sucked into something that the experts didn't understand, and we made a bad situation a lot worse, and then we packed up and left. But for some reason I can't quite explain, that country is the only place that draws me. I don't think it's because of what happened to Mercedes there. It's what it says about the world to me, about the way people behave. The pictures I took when I was there the first time are some of the best I've ever taken in my life. All I did for the most part was concentrate on faces. The whole history of the country is in the faces of those people, in the same way that a lot of our recent history is in the faces of the men we somehow elected. In Lebanon I tried to take my pictures when the people weren't aware of the camera, or the spirit I wanted to capture would be lost. Believe it or not, that's always represented a problem for me. Does a photographer have the right to take someone's picture without his knowledge, without his permission? If it's a matter of permission, then what you get is a posed picture, and a posed picture is an act no matter how you pose the subject. Karsh does a great job with photo-portraiture, but he always reserves in advance his right to choose the posed picture that he prefers. It's still a posed picture, but it's *his* posed picture, and he makes sure he picks the one that looks least posed. But when you take a photograph of someone without his permission or even his knowledge, it's in a way an intrusion, a kind of violation, something like voyeurism, isn't it? I read somewhere that the American Indians always objected to having their photographs taken for that reason. They thought that a photographer was stealing their souls from them when he put them on film. And, of course, they were right. All the Indians I've seen in photographs look like they have faces of stone. There's no soul there. Sometimes you get a glimpse of it in the eyes, but that's rare. And the same holds true for all posed pictures. The soul's gone. You're left with a lot of false surfaces.

"When you get right down to it, Tom, every photographer's a kind of thief. We all are. We're soul-stealers, every one of us. I suppose you can make the case that all artists do that, but we photographers do it without any degree of abstraction. Our perspective—our perspective through the lens—isn't a spiritual perspective. It's just a perspective of distance and angle and concern for the light. If you're lucky once in a while, you get a glimpse of the face beneath the mask. I think I've done that with some of my war photographs. I somehow can justify being a thief with a lens in a war situation because war breaks all the rules in the book anyway. Ansel avoided the whole problem by photographing mountains and flowers and lakes and all those different skies. Portraits by Adams. Great photographs, great photographer at work, great mountains and flowers and lakes and skies, but no people. When you're photographing people—people in motion—you face a different set of problems, and my interest has always been with people, particularly people in adverse circumstances. That's where the drama is. I want to photograph their faces.

"I must have thousands of negatives and prints in my studio, Tom, of faces, just faces, faces from everywhere. And in my way of seeing things a face isn't something that starts from the chin and works up to the top of the head. There are times when the face includes the neck, the chest, the whole body. You have to decide where the face stops. With some women the entire body is a face, and you don't really see them until you see them that way. With others the face is in the way they move their hands or the way they hold them. With some people the face is in the feet.

"But to get back to what I was saying—every photograph I've ever taken, good or bad, stays with me. They're mine. In some instances a photograph may be regarded as a great piece of work, but it's still a theft. You might even say that all my negatives and prints are just stolen goods. And that bothers me from time to time, honestly. What Mercedes said comes back to haunt me. For her, life always came first. And if life does come first, what am I but some kind of poacher on life? I've let the end justify the means. It's a sensitive point. Of course, I'm not as far gone as some lens hounds I know, some of the real paparazzi. For them a photograph's a shot. Just a shot. What they're saying, whether they realize it or not, is that the thing or the person they're photographing is nothing but a target. You get something in your sights, and you pull the trigger. That takes the whole process of photography a stage beyond theft into the minor scales of murder. Actually it's all a blend of theft and murder, and all in a split second. That sounds melodramatic as hell, Tom, but just think of it for a minute. It makes a terrible kind of sense. I've never gone in for it myself, but I know photographers who traipse around after celebrities when the celebrities want to remain incognito and just wait for the exposé shot. Or they come in low in a chopper and take a scope shot of somebody like Jackie O. naked on a beach in Greece or wherever. As soon as they click the shutter, they say to themselves 'Got her.' It's not much different than 'Shot her.'

"That view of photography makes the camera a kind of weapon. It's not a tool any longer; it's a weapon. The object is a target, and what are targets for except to be shot at? I like to think that what I've done with my camera is photography of a higher order, but I don't know. I have my doubts, Tom. It's a thin line. Maybe I'm kidding myself. Maybe I've been a thief, just a thief, or even a petty murderer all my life without realizing it, without admitting it to myself. But what's the answer? I suppose the most ethically correct way of taking photographs is to have in advance the permission of the person you're photographing so that you can take the picture whenever you want without a sense of intrusion. I'm certainly not a thief in that circumstance. The person is respected. I get the picture I want, and my artistic conscience is clean. How's that for a rationalization? But who in the hell takes photographs like that? Nobody. You just keep your camera ready. Targets of opportunity, that's what you wait for. I have a friend who was walking down a street in Pittsburgh with, I think, Weston or Smith, and on the other side of the street there was this legless man who had pieces of tires fixed to the bottom of his stumps. He was making his way down the street on his stumps and using his hands for balance on the sidewalk. Weston had his camera swinging from a strap around his neck (I'm not sure if it was Weston or Smith, but it was one of the two), and he kept talking to my friend, and he just aimed the camera at the cripple and took a picture while he was still talking. A couple of weeks later my friend saw the print that Weston took. There was the legless man just as he remembered. But what he didn't see and what Weston or Smith did see was a one-legged pigeon in the street keeping pace with the man. And there they were, side by side in the photograph forever. Now that's a great still . . ."

Louise has been taking notes on a yellow legal pad while she has been listening to the tape. Now she turns off the recorder so that she can finish transcribing a note on the sheet. It's obvious that her mind is outdistancing her hand, since her hand is making mistakes. As she writes, she cannot help but think that her life has been moving so quickly since she accepted this assignment that she has lost a certain continuity. Listening to the tape and studying the photographs have shown her new ways of looking at familiar things, but she finds herself longing for pauses when she can refocus, question, make up her mind.

Just a week earlier Tom had called her into his office and asked her if she would consider taking on a special project. He then explained how his brother-in-law, Bede Baxter, who had been reported missing in Lebanon for months, was now presumed dead and that he, Tom, wanted to mount a fitting tribute to him. He told her it was commonly agreed that Baxter had become one of the best photographers in the United States during the sixties and seventies and that a documentary would be Baxter's best memorial. As his brother-in-law's only beneficiary (Baxter's wife Mercedes, Tom told Louise, had been killed in Lebanon almost three years earlier), he said that he had access to certain materials (letters, cassettes, published as well as unpublished photographs and memorabilia) that he thought would be appropriate for inclusion in such a memorial and would she, Louise, be interested in putting it together and narrating it.

"How long will the program be?" she asked.

"A half-hour. But we could stretch it to an hour."

"Why don't you do it yourself, Tom? You knew him. Right now he's just a name to me."

"He was my sister's husband, Louise. That might qualify me in one way, but it disqualifies me in another way."

"Are you trying to tell me that I'd be more objective?"

"Exactly."

"How long do I have to think about it?"

"Twenty-four hours. I want to get the project underway as soon as I can."

When Louise finally agreed to make the program, she explained to Tom that what she envisioned was a memorial where Baxter's work would speak for itself. She thought the commentary should be kept to a minimum and that the program should evolve as a series of stills without a human voice to interrupt the experience.

"It would be one focus after another, Tom. This would create a different mood than a motion picture would create. It would give the eye a fix for just an instant, and then this would be followed by another fix. Each photograph would more or less memorize itself in the mind of the person viewing it. That kind of memory sticks, Tom. The viewer sees stills, but he sees stills in motion, one after the other. In fact, that's what I would like to call the program—*Stills in Motion.*"

Tom agreed without argument or reservation, and on the following day he took her to Baxter's house and gave her a room-to-room tour. They started on the second floor. There were two bedrooms and a study there. The main bedroom was in perfect order. The closet still contained a woman's somewhat selective wardrobe, and her shoes were still side by silent side on the floor of the closet. Louise brushed a few of the dresses with her hand. The stirred fabrics released a faint scent of lavender. When she turned away from the closet, she saw several photographs of Baxter and his wife on the dressing table.

"After Mercedes died, Bax never slept in this room," Tom was saying. "At least that's what he said."

"Do you mind my asking how she died? You never told me."

"It happened in Lebanon. She went with him when he took his first trip there in 1982. The story was that they were somewhere in the Chouf, a range of mountains near Beirut. There was a firefight, and Bax was taking pictures. Mercedes was hit. One bullet. A head wound. She died on the spot." Tom paused and looked away at the picture of Mercedes on the dressing table. Finally he said, "Bax came back with the body. He never talked about the incident. Not once. After a while he could talk to me about Mercedes, but he never used the past tense. He might say something like, 'Mercedes likes this time of the year,' or

'Mercedes never forgets anybody's anniversary.' But he never mentioned that last day in the Chouf."

After a long wait Louise tried to return the conversation to what they had been discussing before she had asked about Mercedes. "Is the other bedroom where he slept, Tom?"

"Yes, when he was here. He was overseas a lot. He tried to keep himself busy."

"Why did he want to go back to Lebanon! I'd think that would be the last place . . ."

"If you can understand that, you can understand Bax. Maybe you'll find the answer while you're making this program." Tom looked quickly around the room and then said, "Let me show you the rest of the house another time, Louise. I'm really not up to this now."

"I understand, Tom."

As they drove back to Tom's office, he turned to Louise and said, "Bax had a way of wanting to place himself in jeopardy. Of course, he never saw it as jeopardy. I mean he never admitted that to me. And I don't think he did it for jeopardy's sake like Hemingway or some kind of daredevil. It was just something that came with his job. That's the way he put it. But after Mercedes was killed, he put himself in one dangerous situation after another, and this time it was like Hemingway. I did everything I could to talk him out of it, but I couldn't."

"Did they have any children?"

"No. They wanted children. It was just one of those things. They doctored, did everything."

"Did it affect the way they felt about one another?"

"I don't understand . . ."

"Did they . . . did he regret not having children?"

"They both regretted it. But it didn't weaken what they felt for one another. In fact, it had just the opposite effect. They were really only happy when they were with one another."

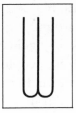

2

WAKING, LOUISE GRABS THE ARMS of the swivel chair and sits rigidly upright. The yellow legal pad slips from her lap and lands flat on the floor. She looks at her watch. Ten minutes short of midnight. She retrieves the legal pad from the floor and edges it onto the desk beside the photographs. Glancing down at the tape recorder, she sees that one side of the cassette ran out while she slept. She reverses the tape almost to the beginning and lets the part she's already heard repeat itself. She realizes suddenly that she has gotten used to Baxter's voice, has grown comfortable with it, has found herself thinking more and more about the man, his wife, and the closed-off bedroom. Was it devotion or morbidity? Regardless, there was something about the act that Louise admired.

She cannot help but compare the marriage of Baxter and his wife with her marriage to Harry. The contrast makes her frown. She had assumed that she and Harry would become "the best of friends" after they were married, but it never happened. She often wondered what the mystery was that made a man and a woman good friends. She never found an answer. When she married Harry, she had hoped that a tenacious devotion would grow between them and bond them. Less than a month after the wedding she realized that such a devotion was not there, had never been there, could never be there.

All that mattered to Harry, really mattered, was the sportswear business. When he talked about sportswear, he gave Louise the impression that something within him was about to ignite.

"Louise," he exclaimed one evening after dinner, "I have an idea that will revolutionize the sportswear business. You know the megabusiness that's grown up around jogging, don't you? Jogging shoes, jogging shorts, jogging sweat suits, jogging sweatbands and the rest. Well, people are getting a little sick of having to jog in all kinds of weather. It takes a real jogger to keep up the habit in the winter. And, besides, as a fad it's starting to wear off. Well, I talked with a football coach the other day, and he mentioned to me that he conditions his team by making them hop every day. One hundred hops on both feet, then fifty on the right, then fifty on the left, then another hundred on both feet. He told me he hasn't had a knee injury in more than fifteen years. It's great for the knees. Now here's the angle." He leaned forward, his eyes glistening. "You don't have to go outside to hop. You can hop in your own game room or in the hall or even in the kitchen. So the weather is never a factor. You can just hop wherever you happen to be. Now, if they can develop shoes and all the rest of that stuff for joggers, why can't we develop a line for hoppers? Shoes with a special pad in the sole? Hopping shorts and tops with the right cling?"

Louise listened patiently. She never discouraged him, but eventually each of his new ideas to "revolutionize" the business glowed brightly and then fizzled like a skyrocket. With every passing month she tired of conversations that dealt only with profit and loss, and their predictable social life of costume parties and bridge foursomes left her with more of a sense of sadness than a feeling of exhilaration.

The fact gradually became clear to her that she really did not love Harry. She trusted him, understood him, understood him perhaps too well, so well that she felt he could never surprise her, and she feared that a life without the potentiality of surprise was a life that would eventually be fatal to whatever did exist between them.

When it came to lovemaking, she simply let Harry make love to her. She did her best not to leave him frustrated. She let herself be satisfied, but there was never a feeling of fulfillment in it. Letting herself be satisfied was not what she craved. What she wanted more than anything else was a wanton giving of herself in an act she could direct but not control. She wanted to be immolated, not merely eased.

Being satisfied by Harry was never anything like that. She let her climaxes happen while she kept her eyes open.

"We ought to try all the different positions, Louise. What's there to lose?" he said one night.

"Harry, how many can there be?"

"A lot. And there are variations."

"But it all ends the same way."

"Louise, sometimes I don't think you have any imagination."

After one of their midnight conversations, Louise could not sleep. The realization that she was living a lie overpowered her. She was a wife, but the concern and affection she felt for Harry were not a synonym for love by her standards. Her life did not consume her. It became more and more difficult for her just to get through a day. The hands of all the clocks moved so slowly. Harry in the meanwhile sensed no change in her. He seemed to draw strength from the very routines that were beginning to suffocate her. Louise saw that he needed her much more than she needed him, and she knew that any kind of separation or rupture would leave him not only bereft but devastated. She hoped that things would change, that Harry would change. At times he was like an adolescent around her. More than once when he tried to make love to her and found her totally unresponsive, she would hold him while he wept uncontrollably, his tears cold against her warm breasts. In those moments she knew that leaving him would make her feel that she had ruined his life in a way for which he was not to blame.

She lived that way for more than a year. She learned to become a convincing actress, but weekly she took more and more aspirin for headaches she could not avoid or endure. She began to think that she was losing her mind.

"Harry," she said one night in a whisper, "are you asleep?"

"No. What's wrong?"

"Harry, I have to tell you something. I have to . . ."

"What is it, Louise?"

"I'm not the one for you, Harry. There's no other way I can say it. I can't live like this anymore."

"Jesus Christ!"

"I've been holding it in for too long, Harry. You have to understand."

"Understand?"

"I'm leaving, Harry. If I don't, I don't know what will happen."

He flung off the blankets and sat crouched on the edge of the bed. He tilted slightly to one side. Crouched and askew, he looked as if he had just been shot. Louise waited. Then without a word he left the room. She heard him go downstairs, heard him slam one door after another.

"In the middle of the night I've got to hear something like this, for Christ's sake! Right out of the blue. Just like that." More slamming. "God damn everything about you, Louise. Do you hear me? God damn everything about you!"

It was almost an hour before he returned to the bedroom. He looked as if he were undecided whether he should be hurt or angry. Louise braced herself for both, but she got neither. Instead he eased himself into bed beside her and began to stroke her side.

"Don't, Harry. Please. It's—"

"Just let me please you, Louise. That's not too much to ask. It'll take care of everything."

"Harry, it's not that. Please, stop that. It will just make things worse."

"Well, damn you, Louise. Damn you!"

She thought for a moment that he was going to hit her, but instead he sat again on the edge of the bed and sobbed. The sobbing seemed more forced than natural, but Louise could not be sure. She knew though that everything was over for her, and she hoped that in time he would come to realize that.

She packed and left the following day and moved in with an aunt for whom she had a special affection and who had understood her since childhood. Within a month she had gone back to her old job with Tom at the city's public television station. For months Harry kept telephoning her at the station, occasionally waited for her after working hours, and once came to her aunt's apartment . . .

Bax's voice on the tape recorder eases Louise back from the spell of her memories of Harry. She looks directly at the tape recorder as if watching the source of the voice brings her closer to the person. She is not concentrating on the words, just the tone of the voice. After a few moments she retrieves the yellow legal pad from the desk and listens.

". . . not an art. Okay, photography may not be an art, but it's a lot more than a skill. At its best it's almost like poetry. I really mean that, Tom. A good photograph is not just an image, an appearance on paper. It's something permanent you've captured in passing, something that's indelible. You lift it out of time and print it on paper forever. It's what happens when the soul of something or someone or some place suddenly shows through, suddenly reveals itself. And at just that instant there's a man or a woman on hand with a camera. And a photograph is made, and there is something in that picture that stays in the present tense for all time to come. That's the poetry of it, Tom. It gives the person who sees the photograph an image that's perfectly clear. And we all need that clarity. Any optometrist will tell you that the brain demands a single, clear image. The brain's never satisfied with fuzzy perceptions. And the soul makes the same demand. It wants a single, clear image of another soul. Do you know the work of Cartier-Bresson, Tom? I know him personally, and I respect him as a master of the art of the camera. Somehow he has the gift or the luck to be where life just happens to happen, and he's quick enough and unobtrusive enough to get what's happening on film. He does it less and less now, but years ago he was superb. I can look at his photographs for hours, and every second of every minute of every one of those hours is always the first time I'm really seeing what I'm looking at. He's a real poet, that man. He's not a poet in the same way that Ansel or the way my friend Gisèle Freund is, but he's a poet in a way that nobody else is. No doubt about that. He respected the mystery of people, the mystery of the moment.

"Today there are so many young photographers who have all the equipment that money can buy and all the training and the rest, but they don't have the eye, and their pictures are just flat. No mystery. They remind me of all those new filmmakers in California and New York. They're into 'cinema.' And technically they're outstanding. They know all about special effects. They know how to shock an audience, especially a young audience, which means an audience that's easy to trick. But no matter how good they are technically and how much they know about depth of field and the rest, they lack the main thing. They don't know the first thing about telling a story. And that's what you have to know how to do if you're going to make a movie. A story is more than special effects. A film has to have a story line in the same way that a song has to have a melody line. That's where the soul is. What I like about stills is that they can tell a whole story in a single focus. And if the photograph is good, then anyone who sees it will feel what the photographer felt when he took the picture. Isn't that what poetry's all about, Tom? A poet stops long enough to give something one hard look, one hard dose of pure attention. And that's just what a photographer does. If the picture isn't good, then what Capa said once is probably the best explanation of what's missing—*the photographer wasn't close enough.* But if you can get close enough and you have a good eye, then the picture probably will be as good as you and the camera can make it. And then when you or anybody else looks at the picture, you get the pleasure of seeing something already seen. And that's often when you really see something. The second time around. Not just look at it, but see it . . ."

While listening to the last few sentences on the tape, Louise has been sorting through a stack of black-and-white glossies on the desk. They are all face shots of the same woman, and Louise senses almost by reflex that all of the pictures are of Baxter's wife, Mercedes. She stops the tape recorder in mid-sentence and begins to study the photographs, one by one. The woman seems always to be smiling through a certain sadness. Her smile is definite but never broad, so that only a hint of her teeth is revealed. It is quite clear to Louise, however, that she is not smiling at or for the camera. In fact, Louise has the impression that the woman was probably indifferent to or unaware of the camera when the photographs were taken. Louise feels that she has seen the woman's expression before, but where? She studies the woman's dark hair, which is brushed loosely back from her forehead without a part. She remembers that Tom told her she had been killed by a bullet in the head, and for an instant a mental image of the fatal wound overlays the photograph. Then she follows the gradually slendering face down to the set and serious jaw, then up to the lips (the top lip slightly thinner than the bottom one), then to the soft eyes that have the same mixture of happiness and sadness, not as a result of mood but apparently as their permanent expression, since all the photographs show her that way.

Louise concentrates on the woman's forehead. She has always been able to learn more about a person's personality by studying the forehead than any other feature. Flipping over photograph after photograph, Louise concludes that the woman is not only thinking, or rather *was* not only thinking when the photographs were taken, but that thinking in a careful, nonrushed way was a habit for her. In every photograph the woman's forehead conveys to Louise the same impression of ongoing, interior meditation.

If Louise can choose one word to describe the woman's expression, her choice would be a word like "benevolence." And at just that instant she recalls where she has seen the woman's expression before. It is a look she has memorized from the Italian madonnas, a blend of maternity and mystery. As she peers again at each photograph, Louise has the feeling that she has known this woman for years. The more she looks, the more she enters into each picture, as if she is looking at pictures of herself or staring at herself in a mirror. It is only when she realizes that she is studying the photographs of a woman who is dead that the photographs begin to wound her, and she has to stop looking at them altogether. At the same moment she remembers the carefully preserved neatness of the bedroom upstairs. Turning on the tape recorder again, she eases herself into the omnipresence of Baxter's voice and shifts the glossies of Mercedes upside down on the desk so that she will not be tempted to look at them again.

". . . for weeks and even longer. Actually I've been thinking for months, Tom, about different ways to make photography prophetic. I mean prophetic in the way that the prophets in the Bible were prophetic. It had nothing to do with knowing or seeing the future. That's hidden from all of us. It just meant seeing the present. The old prophets saw what was happening in the present, and they said so. Now I ask you, Tom, what can do that better than photography? A picture does many things, but one thing it can't do is lie. The camera really sees the present because that's the only time it has, that's all it has to deal with, that's where it exists. The subject is right now and right here all the time.

"Even when Mercedes was alive, I discussed that with her from time to time. I explained to her that I went to places where cruel or inhuman things were happening so that I could get them on film. I just wanted to make pictures of all those things to show that they were undeniable. They were what human beings actually did to one another. That's why she came to Lebanon with me in 'eighty-two. Before that she never stood in my way when I went. I know that it worried her when I'd go to places where there was danger, real danger. Maybe I was too selfish about it. What I really regret right now is that all those trips deprived me of time with her. I just didn't know at the time how little time we had left. In Lebanon we faced the dangers together. I have pictures that would horrify you, Tom. In one of the refugee camps there wasn't a person left alive. The bodies were everywhere. And the heat made them expand like balloons. And sometimes they burst. And when the Israelis came in and rocketed the villages, I would go out just long enough to photograph the workers from the Red Cross and the Red Crescent. And then the planes would come back again and catch the rescuers in the streets. I have one photograph of a young doctor. A rocket had burst in his operating room. He was untouched, but everyone around him was killed. In the picture he's just standing amid all that havoc like a man in a dream. But while I was taking pictures, Mercedes was helping the wounded and taking care of the children and trying to console the old people. That's how I remember her. Now that she's gone, I somehow feel closer to her when I go to places like Lebanon. I can't explain it, but I do. I somehow welcome the danger. Sometimes I even look for it. You might be thinking that I'm out of my mind when I say this, Tom, but honest-to-God I feel closest to your sister when I'm just hanging on to life with my fingernails. That may sound fatalistic and suicidal, but I really feel that way. And at the same time I feel that I'm doing what a photographer like me should be doing, that I'm doing something prophetic. I feel that I'm doing something that I myself must do or else it will never be done, and if it's not done, then the opportunity will be lost forever. It's not as outlandish as it sounds, Tom. It's how I justify my life. For me a good photograph is like a testimony under oath. It's the truth and nothing but the truth. It removes all doubts. My pictures of Lebanon will make Lebanon real for everybody. It will bring war into your soul, into your blood. It will leave nothing to conjecture or faith. It ends all arguments because it forces you to accept the testimony of your own eyes. Suppose, just suppose that photography existed at the time of Christ. And then suppose some photographer in Palestine took a photograph of Jesus Christ on the Sunday after Good Friday. I mean suppose a photograph existed of a man alive three days after he was officially executed. Well, that would take what Christians call the Resurrection out of the realm of faith and make it a matter of fact, a matter of knowledge, something undoubtable. That's my whole philosophy of photography, Tom, more or less. I want to take pictures that no one can deny. And when people see them, they have to react to them one way or another, but they can't wish them away. They can't ever deny what they've seen with their very eyes. What I'm driving at, Tom, is that I'm going back to Lebanon so I can finish the job I started there. I want to get it all on film. And everything that can happen seems to be happening there— from the very best to the very worst. I'll try to stay in touch with you if I can. If not, I'll call you when I get back. If I get back. Take care of yourself, Tom.''

THE FOUR CHAIRS ARE ARRANGED in a semi-circle. Louise is seated in a fifth chair that faces the four. Occupying the chairs in the semicircle are three men and one woman. The man in the first chair is wearing a blue suit that has been tailored elsewhere than in the United States. He has a goatee and a generous mustache. The mustache is brown, but the goatee has both brown and gray hairs in it. The woman to his left is dressed in a simple two-piece gray suit. She sits with both feet on the floor like a graduate of a strict school. She is wearing no jewelry and no cosmetics of any kind. The two men who are sitting to the woman's left are obviously American. The first man looks like the government official he will shortly say he is. He has that riveting and yet inoffensive look in his eyes that is found in foreign-service officers who really believe in public service. What is memorable about him is not his gray hair cut in the style of the forties but the justice of his gray-blue eyes. Beside him sits a younger man in a brown corduroy jacket and khaki trousers. He is wearing white Adidas running shoes. His blond hair is uncombed, and he has the tanned finish of a man who has spent much of his life in the open air.

"All of you have been invited here to participate in this program," Louise is explaining to them, "because you saw or knew Mr. Baxter in Lebanon. We deeply appreciate your willingness to contribute to this memorial to Mr. Baxter. I hope you'll tell me some of your memories of him. You needn't worry about editing your comments or speaking too long. We'll keep the tape running no matter how long it takes, so just say exactly what you remember."

What will survive in the edited tape will be approximately eight minutes of conversation, as follows:

LOUISE: Mr. Ingram, during your stint at the American embassy in Beirut, did you see Mr. Baxter frequently?

INGRAM: Quite frequently. He warned us repeatedly about possible attacks. We took the usual precautions, as you know, but in retrospect they were not sufficient. Baxter really thought that our enemies there were not ideological enemies but circumstantial enemies, and I agreed with him, and I still hold that position even though I'm no longer in government. We are certainly not natural enemies of the

Lebanese people. Americans were always welcome there. It's only lately that Americans are at risk if they go there, and that's been due to a misguided foreign policy. Of course, the politics of the situation did not interest Baxter. I saw many of the photographs that he took when he came to Lebanon with his wife, and they were a chronicle of indiscriminate cruelty on all sides. He took a lot of photographs of children, wounded children. He told me once that all the children in Lebanon were wounded, whether the wounds were visible or not. And his photographs were unforgettable.

LOUISE: Are these some of the photographs you mean, Mr. Ingram? (There is a slow panning across five mounted photographs of children. The most memorable shows two boys standing side by side in the sun. One boy has a crutch under his right armpit, and the other boy has one under his left armpit. The crutches look as if they have been made out of broom handles. One boy is missing his right leg at the hip; the other, his left leg at the knee. Both boys have their free arms around one another's shoulders and are smiling directly at the camera.)

INGRAM: The last time I saw Baxter was a week before he was reported missing.

LOUISE: Thank you, Mr. Ingram. (She turns to the woman in the two-piece gray suit.) Mrs. Shihab, it was you who saw him last, according to reports. Is that correct?

MRS. SHIHAB: Yes. He came to our village. We are, as you know, south of Beirut and in the mountains, and we took many damages during the war and since. We were even shelled by an American battleship, and then by the Israeliens, of course. Do you say Israeliens?

LOUISE: Israelis.

MRS. SHIHAB: Every family in the village had at least one funeral. Even to this day we have no priest because he was killed by fragmentation during one bombing. Mr. Baxter came by himself, and he took many pictures of the families and of the destructiveness, the destroying, how do you say it? It was dangerous for him as an American because there was still bombing from the sea, from the battleship. He came directly to our home because my brother is the mayor of our village. There is a temporary mayor now because my brother is still in Ansar camp in the south. Mr. Baxter was very understanding with me. He wanted to know much of what happened. And then he brought medicine and bandages and blankets that he had in his car. And he left money with me for the people, but it was American money, and the young men, because of what they felt for the Americans, put their spit on the money. Then they took Mr. Baxter into custody with them, and they left the village. At first we heard that he was shot. Then we heard that he was being held for exchange. This is still very common, you know. After that there were many rumors, many reports. When we heard that his body was found burned near Saida, we were very sad, really. They knew him from the passport they found on his body. It was a pity. He was good, and he meant good to us. I could see this from his eyes.

LOUISE: Does that conform to your view of Mr. Baxter, Professor Haddad?

PROFESSOR HADDAD: Almost point for point. He was known to us for many weeks before his disappearance. Not politically, of course. He seemed to consider politics an inferior interest, which is why he managed to move through the country where others could not go or would not dare to go for political reasons. He lived a kind of charmed life for a time. The people he understood best were the forgotten ones, which is what my particular sect has been in Lebanon for many, many years now. Baxter told me that the most difficult thing to photograph is hopelessness. People try to conceal it from the camera, he said. He mentioned to me on another occasion that he wanted to take one photograph that would show that kind of hopelessness to the world. Hopelessness was what he saw in the whole country, in the old and especially in the young. In the old it turned to despair. In the young it turned to violence. Every time someone spoke of a solution, Baxter said that some things had solutions and some things did not have solutions. He mentioned to me privately once that there are wounds you have to live with, like the loss of a past or the loss of a mate. I learned only recently that he had lost his wife in Lebanon. I did not know that when we spoke last. He was resigned to the fact that life had a tragic dimension and that at times people had to accept that for themselves as well as for their country. He said that you had to learn to live wounded.

LOUISE: Mr. Sanders, you're a photographer. You were in Lebanon when Mr. Baxter was there. Is there anything that you would like to add from the point of view of someone in the same profession?

SANDERS: I was in Lebanon on assignment. Bax was there because he wanted to be there, he chose to be there. I had to get pictures on a regular basis for the wire services and for my own magazine. I worked with Biggie Newsome from *Life*. Biggie's still missing, probably dead. I looked on the whole thing as a dirty job. And I was ready to turn my back on it at any moment. Bax saw what I saw, but it had a fourth dimension for him. Maybe it's because his wife was killed there. I don't know. But many times he spoke of what was happening in Lebanon in terms of something else, as if that would help him to understand it better. It was a kind of metaphor for him. Once he told me that Lebanon would symbolize for the eighties and nineties what Spain symbolized in the thirties. He saw in Lebanon the same brutality that existed in Spain before the Second World War, the same blood lust, the same Abel-and-Cain hatred that kept feeding on itself, the same testing ground for a lot of the surrounding countries to try out some new weaponry. And in the last analysis the weaponry came from the Soviets and from Uncle Sam, so there was an international dimension there as well. The only difference between the eighties and the thirties for Bax was that he saw Lebanon as a preface to a different kind of war. He wasn't talking about the nuclear business or the military wars of country versus country. He said that the world was facing the Lebanonization of war—a time of kidnapping, of car-bomb assassinations, of vendettas, of unexpected attacks on innocents in unexpected places. He said it could break out anywhere and that the soldiers in such a war would be indistinguishable from the population because they *were* the population. I never got that involved with him about it, but I've thought a lot about his theory since, and I think he has a point. Bax wanted to show people what that kind of a war was like so that his photographs would be a warning that couldn't be denied. He told me once that he wanted to get one photograph that would show horror in the very act of happening. And he was willing to take the risks to get it. Once I went with him to the south of Lebanon when the fighting was heavy there. We could smell orange blossoms, and there was the scent of bananas too. And then there was the smell of smoke from the fires that the bombs started in the orchards. There was a smell of napalm. And cordite. All mixed together. Orange blossoms and death. It was something I never smelled before, like hell and paradise mixed together forever. Bax's pictures were better than mine. He knew what to focus on. He concentrated a lot on faces, and then he took some pictures that no magazine in the States would print. The French might print them, or the Germans. Pictures of the dead, the violated, the disfigured. Unsanitized stuff. I saw some of the prints. I don't know where they are now, but if someone could come up with those shots or the negatives, that would make one hell of a testament.

L ESS THAN FIVE FEET TALL and slightly bow-legged, the man will be carrying a trombone case. He will look slightly angry, as if he has just had an unpleasant experience with a taxi driver or porter. After passing through the main entrance of the TWA terminal, the man will glance quickly to his left and his right and then hurry into the body of the terminal itself. He will stand under the small bridge that joins the Ambassador's Club to the cafeteria and, after leaning the trombone case against the arch of the bridge and positioning himself beside it, he will scan the gathering of passengers grouped on the curved bench seats in front of the enormous window at the rear of the terminal. Through the window he will notice several parked aircraft and a small helicopter pad. Slowly the anger in his face will vanish. It will be replaced by an expression of total concentration on the passengers in front of the window.

A girl in red jeans will pass the man with the trombone case. She will be carrying a guitar. Returning to the man, she will ask him if he plans to take the trombone case with him on the plane. He will try to ignore her. She will stand for a moment, puzzled by the man's disdain. Then she will say, "Look, I'm just asking to find out if you had to buy a ticket for that thing. I had to buy a special seat for this guitar because I don't trust them with it in baggage, and I think it sucks."

The man will continue to ignore the girl. Shrugging, she will walk away from him and head for the tunnel leading to the departure gates. After watching the girl leave, the man will pick up the trombone case and, still under the bridge, sidle to the opposite side. Still holding the case, he will survey the passengers in front of the window from this vantage point.

Two Franciscan nuns will pass the man and stand for a moment near him until they locate a pair of vacancies on the curved benches. They will seat themselves and talk quietly to one another.

When the shooting starts, both nuns will be hit. One of them will die instantly from a bullet wound just above her right eye. The second one will be struck in the left arm. She will recover completely although for years afterward she will suffer from periodic nightmares.

4

BEING BIGGIE WASN'T HARD FOR ME. I stayed Biggie Newsome for more than five months. There was nothing to explain, and no one suffered because of it. Biggie had nobody. Father and mother dead. No brothers or sisters and never a wife. All in all, it was just a matter of lifting his passport from his body, changing the photographs, planting mine on him or what was left of it on what was left of him. After the napalm and the other stuff hit us, I saw him dead and burned along with the rest of the irregulars from the village that had us in tow. Somehow—I don't know how and will never know how—the fire missed me completely. God knows how, unless Mercedes was looking out for me. Someone had to be looking out for me for the past five months. In that country I think I saw all the violence I ever want to see. I have a lot of it on the film I've been able to salvage. I don't know if the one great shot is there in the lot, but all of them show that what's happening there is no dream. And it's still happening seven times a week and twice on Sunday. Even when you're a witness, it's so hard to believe. You want to deny what your eyes saw and your nose smelled, but you can't because they saw what they saw and it smelled what it smelled, and the senses don't lie any more than a photograph lies. I've always believed that. There's no such thing as a false photograph, only a bad one. I remember the smell of the dead below Beit Meri. And I saw what must have been done to them before they were dead, and that was a memory in itself. I have a lot of that on film although I don't know if I have the stomach to develop what I have. I keep reminding myself that they were genuine people once, genuine honest-to-God people and not the carcasses they were when I saw them. Even Biggie told me that he never saw anything like it, and Biggie had seen a lot in Afghanistan and in Vietnam. I've lived for less than half a year now on Biggie's passport, and it's only twenty-four hours ago that I decided to come back to life. I mean to come back to life as myself. The people at our embassy were good about it when I asked them if they'd keep the story to themselves, at least until I got back to the States. I'll release it there myself. I might even ask Tom to help me do it. He's good at that. I still can't say why

I decided to come back unless everybody has the right to come back from the dead at least once in his life. I was as good as dead to the whole world, and it wasn't just because I was reported to be dead but because I was really dead from the inside out. A man's by all rights dead when he doesn't want to wake up and shower and shave and get dressed and face people. There was no real reason for me to want to do that anymore. Life itself wasn't reason enough without Mercedes. Every day just wasn't reason enough for me because there was no one to share a damn thing with. It was like my life stopped when she died. I could never think of my life without her. Even before we were married, we felt married. Marrying was something we both knew would happen, and when it did, it was like a prophecy coming true. It seemed as natural as growing or breathing. When she died, I felt a certain power go out of me the way that a man who has suffered a stroke feels a certain power go out of him forever. After that there was only work, working alone, working and being alone. Working became its own solitude, and there was nothing I could do to keep myself from waking from the same nightmare where all I heard was Mercedes in the darkness. And it was always the same nightmare. Mercedes would be screaming at me. She would be telling me that we had enough pictures, that there was no more time, that we had more than we needed, and then there was the sound of that rifle shot, and all at once I'd be sitting on the edge of the bed with the sweat coming off me like shower water. One night my hair was so wet that I had to get up and dry it with a bath towel before I could lie down again. And that happened four or five times a month. I keep asking myself why I didn't listen to her and stop. I had enough pictures. Why was it that she knew when enough was really enough and not a hair more, and I didn't? Months later when I had the courage to develop the rolls that I took in Lebanon, I finally narrowed it down to the one roll that was in the camera when Mercedes was hit. I found thirty-five usable stills and one blank. That was the last one on the roll, the one I took after she asked me to stop, the one I didn't have to take. If I hadn't taken it, then Mercedes might be alive today. I don't give a damn if the other stills won all the awards in the history of American photojournalism and if they're in all the textbooks in the world. They cost me my wife. They cost me my life. Everybody tries to tell me that it wasn't my fault, and I do my best to believe it, but it doesn't help. Every day I live with that. Even since she's been gone, I've gotten into the habit of thinking that life is like keeping money in the bank. I've kept holding back and holding back, keeping myself away from people. I mean keeping my thoughts from people, even from Tom. I don't want my life to get tangled up with other lives anymore. So I've kept it in the bank. What I didn't realize was that I started to rot as soon as I started to think that way. I had no one to give my life to, so I hoarded it. Mercedes was always doing just the opposite when she was alive. She was always helping somebody else, always anticipating what someone else needed, and she was always more alive because of it even though she never thought of doing anything for that reason. It just ended up like that. They say you have to lose your life to find it. She was always losing her life for somebody else, especially for me. I can count on one thumb the people I know who understand what that means, but she knew what that meant without giving it a thought. I really wanted to lose myself back in Lebanon, but it was for the wrong reason. I wasn't doing it for anybody else. I was doing it for myself. I guess that I wanted to kill whatever it was inside of me that kept remembering, that wouldn't defend me against the nightmares. Or maybe I thought I would find a good, quick death there. Maybe I just wanted to die the way Mercedes died. And to die where she died. But you just can't die when you want to no matter how real the danger is. After three months I finally faced up to that. I was trying to write myself out of the script on my own terms, and life wasn't cooperating. And so I decided that wanting to die or hoping to die by accident wasn't the answer. Life just wouldn't oblige me by being my executioner, so I came back to life as myself. I suppose I'll call Tom from New York when we get in and tell him the whole story before I tell anybody else. Or maybe I'll just go home and call him from there. Maybe that would be better. It would avoid all the fuss at the airport and all the rest. Together we'll find a way to release the story to the public so there won't be a big splash. I'll just tell him that I didn't want to be anonymous any longer, that I thought I could get better pictures if no one knew who I was, and that I'm sorry about the whole plan now. People might accept that. As myself or as Biggie the killing was no less terrible, and the sound of the bombs and the sound of the rockets no different. And seeing the burnt scraps of what used to be people was, God help me, no different. I'll be seeing those things every time I remember. And all that I want is for everybody to see those memories through the eye of my camera. They'll see a chronicle of murder in stills, of suffering in stills, of desperate love in stills, and there will

even be stills of innocence in the midst of that hell. There's
a world in my camera that no one knows. And that world
is going to be my legacy. The photographs will do all the
talking, and if that kind of talk is not loud enough, then
there's nothing that's loud enough. If somebody else can do
it better, that's okay by me. There's enough out there for
all the witnesses in the world. And there's no competition.
It's amazing what you get used to in a war. I remember once
that I was in a village, and there was a woman named Shihab
who was serving kibbee and the flat village bread they bake
in the mountains. While we were eating, we could hear the
shells passing over our heads. But we kept on eating, and
then there would be a thud and a boom farther up the
mountain. We just shrugged and thought about the food
since we weren't on the receiving end of that shell. At the
time, you never thought that someone farther up the mountain had chewed his last serving of kibbee and bread because the shell found him. You just didn't think that way.
You adjusted. You got used to it. You learned that you
could get used to anything. There was another time when
I was having coffee with Biggie in Hamra. Behind us there
was a stucco wall and behind the wall was a house. We could
hear a little girl singing a nursery song in Arabic behind the
wall. Then we both noticed a white Land-Rover coming
down the street a little too quickly even by Beirut standards.
When the car was abreast of us, a guy on the passenger side
lobbed a grenade right over our heads and into the yard
behind the wall. Then there was an explosion, and after a
second or two the stones and dirt and a whole lot of other
debris came down like the wrong kind of rain all over the
table and the coffee cups and over our heads and shoulders.

While Biggie was shouting that we should get the living hell out of this nuthouse of a city, I stood up and slipped through a new hole in the stucco wall and across what was left of the patio inside. I saw the little girl in a blue dress on the ground. Her legs were bent under her in a way that was unnatural, and the tricycle she must have been riding was on top of her, and everything looked at first glance like a bad but common accident. Except the little girl had no head. There was no head at all where her head was supposed to be. And behind her was an old man, maybe her grandfather. He was lying facedown, and the blood from a wound in his back was already like a growing circle of spilled paint under him. I went back for my camera that I'd left beside my chair at the table. When I returned to the patio, the blood from the old man's wound was a bigger circle. I took one photograph with the little girl in the foreground and then another with the old man in the foreground. Biggie watched me. He didn't take a single picture, just watched. I took three other pictures for good measure, and then we left. That night he asked me why I'd taken the pictures. I said why not. And that was the end of that. We found out the next day that the fucking grenade was a mistake. The whole operation was meant for some official or other who had a house next door. But he was in Kuwait at the time anyway, so the whole mission, the whole double murder, was a mistake. But I'd gotten a picture out of it. I thought for a few days of what the little girl and the old man must have thought when they saw the grenade come over the wall like a beanbag or a loose ball and how they must have watched it hit and roll a few times and then go off. I thought of them at that moment. That was the kind of war

it was in Lebanon and the kind it still is there, and maybe
it's the kind of war that will be with us from now on. Not
just to the end of the century but from now on. It can be
waged anywhere. All you need is someone with a grievance
and no real concern for his own life. And all he needs to
declare war is a bomb that he has strapped to his side (and
it might even be some kind of nuclear bomb since the
technology is available for everyone now) while he walks
through the Paris Bourse or somewhere in downtown
Washington or New York or even in Moscow or in London. And then he stops and attacks. That's what happened
to the Marines in Beirut. One man in a truck took a couple
of hundred Marines with him to kingdom come, and one
Marine colonel told me that it was the largest nonnuclear
explosion in the history of war. And if that kind of thing can
happen in a military area where people are more or less
prepared for it, it can happen a hell of a lot easier in the
middle of Grand Central terminal, and then you have not
hundreds but thousands being blown apart. It takes as much
strategy to do that as to kill a little girl and her grandfather
behind a stucco wall in Beirut by mistake because the real
target was somewhere in Kuwait, and the bomber didn't
know the difference and didn't really give a damn anyway.
It was just a wasted grenade to him. There were more
where that came from. And a month later they got the guy
after he came back from Kuwait. He was killed with knives
in a most definitive way, and then they packed him tongue-
less and cockless like a piece of carcass beef in the back of
that same old white Land-Rover until the smell was enough
to let the police discover what they were intended to discover in just that way. And if anybody has any doubts about

that incident, I have a photograph of the remains of that official in that trunk, and you can see exactly what the leftovers of a man look like after he's been carved up that way like a steer and left to bloat for a day or so at sea-level in the middle of the summer. That's the kind of war I photographed. I guess that no one but Tom will understand why I had to go there and then why I had to leave. He's like Mercedes that way, the same kind of character. He just listens until he understands, and he wants to understand, he really wants to understand. And that shows in the programs he makes for the tube. He has some real integrity left. He's not like the network whores who'd cancel out their mothers if the ratings told them to do it, and it's all for the greater glory of soap or razor blades or this year's car. I used to think that nothing was worse than war. Loneliness is worse. Put them both together, and suicide presents itself as a kind of solution, or at least as a possibility. I really felt the temptation. And I even started to hope that I would catch a stray bullet through the courtesy or bad aim of some stranger, and then everything would be settled once and for all. There was real cowardice for you. And romantic cowardice to boot. I'd seen enough to know that there was a hell of a lot that can happen to you this side of death, like being blinded by a bomb or losing a leg or both arms or having half your face blasted away, and you think hard about what it would be like to end up like that. And then living on doesn't look so bad after all, even if you're lonely. So you think yourself back from suicide a step at a time, and while you're thinking, you notice too many children crutching along on one good leg or one boy moving himself along on no legs at all, and you feel like the coward you've let yourself become in the face of real life. And then, right then, you decide to live and come back to your real self because even the remainder of a life is better than no life at all, and you go on living, and you take a few less chances than you took before. Of course, you still take chances for a good picture because you're a photographer, and there's always the one good picture out there waiting to be taken. I know that's what I'm on this planet to do, and I'm just going to go on doing it because that's the only thing that fulfills me the way that painting fulfills a painter when he's painting. Mercedes was just beginning to understand that when I lost her. She always tried to understand earlier, but she worried so much about me that she never made her truce with the artistic side of what I had to do. She was always glad when I got back in one piece. In those days she just saw it as a job I did, a way to earn a living. Then later she started to see it as a kind of vocation. And that's what it still is for me. I couldn't turn away from it if I wanted to. It keeps me sane, not just busy. Photography's an art no matter how the purists or the critics disagree about that. Most of them never took a real picture in their lives. And it doesn't matter if you're using a little Kodak or a Hasselblad or a Leica or the king of them all, a Nikon. It's what you get on the negative that matters. And if you're in the middle of a war, it's the most dangerous art of all. And that's how it was every day in Lebanon. It wasn't a question of going to the front. The front was all around you, but you couldn't put your finger on it. And you had to be careful when you held a camera because some trigger-happy kid might mistake it for a weapon and let fly a round or two. Twice that happened to me, and I just thanked God that whoever was shooting was a lousy shot. But then most of the ones with guns were lousy shots. Kids with no real training in marksmanship. And for them marksmanship wasn't that important. Holding the weapon was all that mattered to them. And firing the weapon mattered to them even more, although most of the time they didn't know what they were firing at—it excited them like sex. In a firefight I'd see them go out into the middle of an intersection and start shooting from the hip in the general direction of where they thought the enemy ought to be, and then they'd slip back into the shelter of the building where they were hiding, and they'd be smiling and sweating like a thief who's just pulled off a heist and a getaway or like someone who's just had sexual intercourse with a queen. It's the same expression you see on the faces of people who are driving powerful automobiles. They're turned on by having all that power waiting for a touch of their toe on the accelerator to let it out of prison, and the excitement goes through them like electricity. A camera in hand can give some photographers that same false sense of power. I know a lot of them who use it like a machine gun. I remember once I was with Biggie. He asked me to come with him for some pictures of Marilyn Monroe when she was visiting New York. There were photographers from the newspapers and from *Life* and *Time,* and there were stringers for the tabloids and, of course, that wolf pack from *Stern* and *Paris Match* and a whole cadre from Italy. It was like the Marine Corps firing line at Parris Island. The clicking never stopped for a second. Even when the questions started, the shooting went on and on like a barrage, and the flashes kept going off like flares. I felt ashamed of my profession. From then on I decided I would take the pictures I wanted to take for my own reasons and for no one else's. I could spend a whole day photographing an arch or the knob of a door or the way sunshine slanted through a bedroom. Before I married Mercedes, I photographed a lot of nudes, but never as cheesecake. I wouldn't photograph a woman's body until I taught myself to see it as geography. Then you really see the beauty of it. I remember one girl who said that she'd never posed nude before in her life but that she needed the money. It took me more than a half an hour to make her relax. Actually she never really relaxed, but it turned out all to the good because a certain tension never left her body. It made her entire body more alert, and the light caressed her like a breeze. I only took about three frames, that's all. But one of them was perfection. Her black hair is falling loose, and she is looking up at me with the eyes of an Indian. And her whole body has come to attention. The face of her body is looking at me or at whoever is looking at the photograph. It's amazing. When I was in Lebanon, I trained myself to see everything I photographed as geography. That's the only way I could turn the camera on some of the things I saw. I kept telling myself that these were not dead men and dead women and dead children but parts of a composition. I got so good at it that I began to wonder if I was still human. How could I forget that what I was framing in my lens was somebody's wife or brother or father or grandmother or grandfather? That's when I learned that I was almost dead inside. If human beings were just so much unburied meat, then I was in bad shape. I was as dead as they were. And I thought of Mercedes, and I wanted to come back to life, back to my house, back to the States. The last thing I wanted was to end up in some alley in Lebanon, and I didn't want to be buried in a pit of lime like Biggie. And so here I am, heading back to New York. The last time I came back, I was bringing Mercedes back with me to bury her. And it's like yesterday. It's like this minute. It's still like this minute.

WHENEVER HARRY HAD something serious to discuss, he called Louise. During their two-year separation she became accustomed to the calls and occasional visits. He would discuss a lingering mutual bank account which he thought they should phase out, a new client, a girl he met in New York who seemed to have a lot in common with him and what did Louise think of his seeing the girl again. Louise said that she saw no problem, but the next time she saw Harry she learned that the girl barely remembered their first meeting and was being transferred to Los Angeles anyway.

This call sounded different. Harry sounded apprehensively happy on the phone, as if there was something that he wanted to share with Louise before he shared it with anyone else. Louise suspected another attempt at a reconciliation. She listened for clues, detected none and agreed to meet Harry for dinner. She still felt a residual guilt for having left him as she did, and seeing him occasionally and listening to his problem of the moment eased her conscience somewhat. She did these things unselfishly, hearing Harry out with almost religious attention as if her attention were a matter of conscience with her or even a debt she felt she still owed to him. And she also knew that her judgment meant a lot to Harry. It always had . . .

They are halfway through dinner. Louise, at Harry's insistence, has been talking about her work on the Baxter memorial film and explaining how she has had to edit a lot of material down to size. She talks with an animation he has rarely seen in her, as if the job has now become a deep part of her life and not merely another assignment. What she does not tell him in so many words is that Baxter the man as well as his photographs and the story of his life have moved her to the point where she feels she has become an authority on all phases of the subject.

"We're leaving the photographs in black and white and splicing them into the interviews or other footage," she explains, "so that there is a continual movement throughout the film from color to black and white and back to color again."

"Louise," says Harry when there is a pause. He puts down his knife and fork.

As soon as Louise hears him say her name, she knows that Harry has not really been listening to her but only preparing himself for this moment. She should have guessed it. It was a sales strategy he had once described to her. Let the client talk about what is most interesting to him so that he reveals himself, then come at him with your pitch before he can put his guard up again.

"Louise," Harry repeats, fidgeting with his cuff. "Are we all washed up, the two of us? Is everything over?"

"Please, Harry," Louise responds evenly and calmly. "I don't want to go through this again. Don't make me, please."

"But it's hard to live in suspense, Louise. I still feel the same about you. You know that."

"There's no suspense, Harry," says Louise, looking into his eyes. "I'll do anything for you. I mean that. But it doesn't go beyond that. In fact, it doesn't go further than that with anybody. The problem isn't you, Harry, believe me. The problem is me."

"You never gave me a chance to solve that problem for you, do you know that?"

"Please, Harry. Let's not start again. Not here. The evening's been nice. Let's not spoil it by ending it this way."

They finish the meal without exchanging another word. Later, while Harry is driving her home, he puts his hand near hers, and she takes it out of an old instinct. She feels Harry's fingers tighten around her own.

"Can I show you something at the apartment? Our apartment?" he asks.

"Now?"

"It won't take ten minutes."

"You're not playing another game with me, are you, Harry?"

"No, no, nothing like that. This is on the level. Ten minutes, that's all."

"All right. Ten minutes."

Later Louise will ask herself why she acquiesced so easily, and she will never be able to answer the question honestly. Now as they head toward the apartment that she and Harry shared for more than three years, she feels a comfortable nostalgia come over her. She remembers how the two of them would come back to the apartment from a film or a play or a concert along these very streets, and for a moment she takes a certain security and even a measure of solace in the memory. She is still relishing that feeling of security and solace as Harry pulls the car up to the front of the apartment, as he leads her to the disquietingly familiar door that leads into the vestibule that leads into the all too familiar living room, as he takes her coat. She sits down on the familiar sofa and waits for Harry to tell or show her whatever it is he has brought her here to let her hear or see.

"Are you sitting down on the sofa?" Harry asks as he closes the hall closet door where he has just draped her coat on top of his own.

"Yes."

"You haven't turned around yet, have you?"

"No," Louise answers, resisting the temptation to turn.

"Don't. Not yet. Not before I tell you."

Harry crosses the room. He stands directly in front of her and smiles. "Are you ready?" he asks.

"Ready."

"All right. One. Two. Three. Turn."

Louise turns slowly and looks at the wall several yards behind the sofa. She sees, built into the wall and flanked by walnut cabinets, a stereo system that resembles the interior of the cockpit of a transoceanic jet. The entire facade is a dazzle of dials and knobs and numbers and equalizers. Harry observes it like a man in hypnosis. It is as if there is almost a sexual attractiveness in the machinery for him.

"Well," he asks, smiling, "what do you think?"

"When do we taxi and take off?"

"It's the ultimate, Louise. State of the art. When I have the music going, it's like I'm sitting inside the orchestra. Right inside. And with earphones it's an experience in outer space."

Louise smiles indulgently and tries to look impressed. She is thinking that this could not be more typical. With "things" Harry always went to the final limits of perfectibility. His Corvette was factory-made in the silver color of his choice. His sunglasses were always the "best and the latest." It even used to carry over into their sexual relations. Sensing that Louise, as he told her on one occasion, was "slow" but not understanding the reasons why, Harry invested in various stimulatory rubber toys that he thought would help. Louise was repulsed by them, but she was amazed to learn that such things actually existed. Rejected on that salient, Harry countered by bringing home certain pornographic cassettes. He tried to mollify Louise by explaining to her, with the same sensitivity he exhibited when discussing the intricacies of his Corvette with his mechanic, that the cassettes were only a visual aid. They might help to make things happen. When he finally overcame her refusals by sheer persistence, he was angry to discover that the explicitness of the cassettes, while stimulating him, only depressed her. For days afterward she even refused to talk to him.

"This stereo must have cost you a few paychecks, Harry," says Louise, facing him again.

"A few, but it was worth it. You know me, Louise. Always a new toy." He walks over to the stereo controls, touches and turns a few dials and then stands back while the room gradually swims with a slow tango.

"May I have this dance?" asks Harry, returning to her side.

"Harry, you said ten minutes. I have to get to bed. Really, I do. I'll be editing film all day tomorrow, and then I have some research to do at Baxter's house again. The program is in its final stages, and I want to finish strong."

"One little dance? When did dancing ever tire you out, Louise?"

Louise lets his arm encircle her. She follows him woodenly through the first few steps, and they continue in time with the music. The South American music transports her out of the apartment and into the world of some of Baxter's photographs. She had spent the entire afternoon studying a Latin American series of stills. During the weeks of research she has discovered that Baxter's pictures have established themselves in her mind as her most reliable frames of reference. They have created a norm of reality for her against which she tends to measure everything else. She is screening the photographs in her imagination one by one and is only casually aware of Harry's hand making soft circles in the small of her back and then slowly down. She lifts his hand up, but it returns to the small of her back and starts sliding down her right buttock as much by gravity as by choice.

"Harry, please. You don't have to let your hand go there."

"It just goes by itself, Louise."

"Please, Harry."

"I've missed you a lot, Louise. Can't you feel how my hand has missed you?"

"Harry, I don't want the evening to end like this. With bad feelings. Or a tug of war. Or a fight. We've been through all that. Let's leave well enough alone."

"I've missed you a lot," whispers Harry and kisses her on the forehead and then on the lobe of her right ear.

"But we're not the way we were anymore, Harry."

"Who says so? We're human beings, aren't we? We've been through a lot together. We can't shut off our feelings, can we? You're as human as I am, Louise. Why don't you admit it?"

"Harry, for God's sake." Louise already knows that she is losing this argument. She feels she should never have come here. She senses the quickening of Harry's desire for her in the tenseness of his fingers on her hip, and his touch has started to awaken in her a hunger that, when alone, she could control simply by distracting herself.

"Come on, Louise," Harry is saying in a slow purr. "What is there to lose? We're still married, aren't we? We're not doing anything wrong."

Louise does not answer. Taking her silence as consent, Harry begins to undo the buttons on the back of her blouse, and she resists him briefly before abandoning herself to whatever he is doing. He eases her out of her blouse, undoes her brassiere carefully and then helps her out of her skirt and shoes and other underthings. Naked, she lets herself be embraced tightly and listens to the tango that is softening to a close on the stereo. Strangely, she feels her own desires diminishing as Harry's intensify, and she almost decides to reverse what has already happened or rather what she has already let happen. But then, out of lethargy or a simple unwillingness to deal with the unpleasantness she knows will follow her resistance, she lets the idea pass out of her mind.

Harry edges her back to the sofa and down before he hurriedly undresses and joins her there. He acts like a man in a race. He kisses Louise on the lips, the cheeks, the nipples and then on the lips again. His hands read the soft Braille of her body over and over. When his fingers travel toward her loins, Louise stops him with her free hand.

"Nothing for me, Harry. You go ahead and do whatever you feel like doing, and if something happens for me without any preliminaries, okay. If not, okay too."

Harry frowns but continues to kiss her. Louise can feel his growing hardness against her thigh. Moments later, when she is lying under him on the sofa, she observes his thrustings as if she is somehow removed from the entire scene. And she continues to feel removed as Harry shudders with a climactic push that tenses and then eases him like the passing of a delicious pain. For a moment or two he remains on top of her, heaving with the strain of his efforts and sweating noticeably.

"Anything happen, Louise?" he asks huskily. "For you, I mean?"

"No, Harry. I'm just not the happening kind. But you can't say I didn't warn you."

"Didn't you feel anything at all? Not a thing?"

"It's not that way for me, Harry. But I really don't want

to talk about it, all right? Don't blame yourself. I'm just one of those girls who's still on Mountain time when it comes to sex. You're on Daylight Saving."

Without another word Harry lifts himself off her and, shaking his head from side to side as if coming to terms with a difficult and possibly hopeless problem, strides into the bathroom. Louise watches him go. All that she thinks of for a second is that she is watching a naked man who was once her husband walk into his own bathroom. Then she hears the shower. One minute, two minutes, three minutes, four minutes. Finally the sound of the shower stops. Louise raises herself on one elbow, then straightens into a sitting position. She wonders if they have stained the fabric of the sofa, but she does not check.

She is already back into her underclothes when Harry bursts out of the bathroom and almost marches toward her. He has combed his hair carefully, and she can detect the scent of shaving lotion or cologne freshly applied. He stands naked in front of her, presenting his body like a statement in itself.

"A lot of women would have come two or three times by then, Louise. A lot of women . . ."

He stands his ground, waiting for an answer. Louise continues to dress. She tugs up her pantyhose, stands and dons her blouse and steps into her skirt. She knows that Harry is spoiling for a reaction from her.

"Harry," she says gently. "I've never been the exploding kind, so just write me off. I tried to tell you that this wasn't a good idea, but you weren't in the mood to take no for an answer. Don't get mad at me, please. I'm too tired to cope with that now."

Louise steps toward him, places her hand on the back of his neck and soothes him as she would a child who has just had a poignant but not mortal disappointment.

"Take me home, Harry," she says. "I need to sleep. I have so much work ahead of me tomorrow."

Harry pulls away from her. He sits on the edge of the sofa and stares down through his slightly spread knees at the floor. He is muttering to himself, but Louise can't understand what he is saying. He remains that way for several minutes. At last he rises and says, "Okay, I'll take you home, Louise." He picks up his clothes where he has thrown them and is dressed in seconds . . .

When they are less than ten blocks from Louise's apartment, Harry, who has not said a word to her since they entered his Corvette, asks, "Louise, do you know why I really wanted to see you?"

Louise is surprised by the question. Having seen the new stereo system in Harry's apartment, she automatically thought that there had been no other reason.

"Do you really want me to tell you?" asks Harry.

"Well," sighs Louise, "I suppose I'd rather know than not know. I thought the main event was behind us."

"I've met someone, Louise. I mean I've really met someone this time."

"Another someone?" asks Louise. She feels sure that Harry is lying, that this is his reprisal for their one-sided lovemaking on the sofa.

"No, not another someone. Not this time. This is pretty real. This is the real thing."

Louise looks with disbelief across the seat at Harry and reminds herself that this is the same man whom she admitted to her body less than thirty minutes before, whose fluid is still inside of her, who made her think that he was overcome by such a need for her, specifically for her, that he couldn't refrain from having her.

"I've been seeing a lot of her for the past month and a half," says Harry. "She spent a couple of nights in the apartment, and everything seems all right between us. No hang-ups. No problems on that level. So I was wondering about marrying her after our final papers, yours and mine, come through next week. In fact, I'd like her to meet you."

Suddenly Louise realizes that Harry has been harboring this story all evening and that it has the ring of truth, Harry's version of the truth, to it. Realizing that, she feels she has been soiled, as if Harry serviced himself at her expense on the sofa as a kind of experiment, a way of making comparisons between her, or rather his sexual moment with her, and Miss New-on-the-Scene. And she complied. She tells herself that she complied without suspecting a thing. The thought of that makes her shrink within herself, and she feels an anger around her heart that frightens her with its fury, as if she has been violated through a trick and, having been used, is now hungry for some kind of redress to make herself feel less sordid.

"Anyway," says Harry, "I wanted to talk this over with you before she and I did anything so that you'd be the first to know about it."

"What's her name?" asks Louise.

"You don't know her, Louise. She's only been in town for the past year. She's from Denver."

"But that doesn't mean that I don't want to know her name. She does have a name, doesn't she?"

"You don't have to ask like that, Louise. Sure, sure she has a name. It's Turnbaugh, Sally Turnbaugh."

To Louise the new pairing seems to go together better than Harry and Louise. Harry and Sally, Harry and Sally, Harry and Sally . . .

"Sally knows all about us, Louise, about our marriage, about everything. And she'd like it if you could come to the wedding. I'll let you know the time and date . . ."

Louise studies Harry as if he has all at once been transformed into a question mark.

"Her brother's a minister, and she said he could marry us in her parent's home in Denver. A small wedding." Harry waits for Louise to say something, but Louise is staring straight ahead. "Well, I did what I promised to do. I told Sally that I'd let you know face-to-face, which is what I'm doing now. But if you can't . . ."

"Harry!"

"Yes."

"Are you listening to what you're telling me, for God's sake?"

"Yes. I'm serious about it. Totally serious."

"Harry, you're crazy. You're absolutely crazy!" She is trying to control herself. "First of all, Sally Turnbull—"

"Turnbaugh, Louise. Sally Turnbaugh."

"Well, Sally Turnbaugh has every reason to hate the ground I walk on, to hate my guts. So let's leave it at that. And after that little exercise back in your apartment, I don't know whether to spit in your face or what. How dare you use me like that? How dare you do that? Why didn't you have the courage and the plain honesty to tell me about Ms. Turnbaugh before you made me believe that you needed me?"

"What difference would that have made?"

"A lot of difference, Harry. A lot of difference to me. And now you're asking me to put my blessing on your wedding as if that's supposed to smooth everything over for the two of you. What in the hell goes through that brain of yours? What kind of a man are you anyway?"

"We never did understand one another, Louise."

"Harry," screams Louise. "Stop the car! Stop it right here before I do something desperate. I can't breathe in here."

"Come on, Louise. Don't get so dramatic—"

"Stop the car right here, Harry! I have to get out. Stop this car, Harry, for the love of Christ or I'm going to jump out!"

Before Harry coasts the Corvette to a halt, Louise has already opened the door. She pivots off the seat and stands clear of the car. She slams the door shut with all her strength. Then she stands perfectly still.

Harry rolls down the window and says, "Louise, we could have done without all this."

"Harry," Louise says, her voice quivering, "don't try to call me or see me anymore. Let the lawyers handle everything. I'll approve what they do. But no more calls, Harry. No visits, no letters, nothing."

S IS ALWAYS THE CASE when he returns from trips, the house seems to have shrunk in his absence. It appears to huddle within itself as if it is trying not to be seen as differing from any other house on the Belgian-blocked street. Even now in the growing darkness the house seems to be diminishing as he looks at it, becoming part of history, fading into a blur like an old photograph.

When he bought the house, it was only because Mercedes liked it instantly.

"It's a house that has a sense of living about it, Bax," she told him. "A brand-new house for me is like a brand-new pair of shoes. You know you're the first wearer, but you don't know if the fit will be good or not. The shoes have to become old shoes before they're really good for you, really yours. It always surprises me that everybody seems to want a house where nobody's lived before. It reminds me of the Holiday Inns. Everything is done to convince you that you're the first one who's ever used the room you're in. You're not the first one, of course. You know that. They know that. But they try to make you think that you're the first. They even put a paper ribbon across the toilet seat. It's as if newness for some people is an end in itself. I'm just not like that. Old roads are the best roads. They have more character. They're more interesting."

After Baxter purchased the house, he and Mercedes did not so much try to remake it as they tried to make it more itself. In some curious way they respected it, and they wholeheartedly tried to accommodate themselves to it. From their first night until their last night together in the house, they always felt at home in it.

Setting his luggage down on the sidewalk, Baxter looks at the facade of the house. It makes him remember how he and Mercedes had once stood where he is now standing and just looked at the house together before they inspected the interior. Her eyes were already alive with both curiosity and anxiety. Then he remembers the last time he saw her, her body so still that he thought of her as a shot wren, her face turned so that he at first did not see where the bullet had struck her, her lips still seeming to be saying forever the last word of her life—his name. And he remembers with a tightening in the back of his throat that it was his persistence in wanting to get one more photograph that made her say what she said just before the bullet found her.

"Bax," she shouted over the sound of the gunfire, "that's enough. Please, Bax."

He concentrates on the windows on the first floor. He sees the white curtains and tan drapes that Mercedes made for them when they first moved into the house. He remembers the times they sat in the living room and listened to Bach or Berlioz or Duke Ellington and played casually competitive games of backgammon. Mercedes was the more tactical player, but victory seemed to have a sour taste for her, and she always gave him the impression that she did not want to press her advantage for fear she might win. He often wondered about that trait in her but never reached any kind of conclusion about it. Baxter did try to exorcise her of this tendency, this "weakness," explaining that this deprived both of them from getting maximum pleasure from the game, but he finally realized that this was part of her nature and that there was no changing her style of play without changing her, and this, he concluded, was manifestly impossible. Of course, there were many games that she could not help but win from him because the cast of the dice made victory inevitable for her, but she always moved quickly on to the next game, telling him in passing that she wished someone would invent a game where victory could be shared equally as in lovemaking. It was a way of hers, and it made Baxter treasure even more his evenings with her with the backgammon board between them because it showed him a side of his wife's nature that he would not have otherwise seen. Later they might read to one another from a book that each was involved in reading at the time, and the sharing of special paragraphs or phrases made the reading more of a duet than a solitary act. Finally Baxter would brew some Mocha Java coffee, grinding the glossy beans in a small grinder that he kept spotlessly clean for just that purpose, and serve it with slices of peeled apple or pear, and they would drink and eat together as the voices of Tagliavini or Edith Piaf or Nat King Cole slowly transformed the room into the mood of the song of the moment, creating an atmosphere that was beyond the power of the room to create for itself but somehow made the room more *room* and the house more *house.*

If such a night were on the eve of one of Baxter's trips, Mercedes would try to distract herself from the packed suitcases near the front door where they were waiting side by side like unwelcome accomplices in a drama she hated but could not avoid. At such times Baxter would almost be moved to cancel the trip, as if the prospect of causing Mercedes the hurt that she did her best to conceal was simply too high a price to pay for what he had to do. But in the morning the prospect of the trip and the job at hand would make him forget his hesitancy, and he would leave with his usual jauntiness, but her good-bye smile would stay with him like a kiss for days . . .

Baxter walks along the sidewalk in front of his house to the point where his property line ends. Then he returns and stands beside his luggage. He still concentrates on the white curtains and tan drapes in the living room windows. Slowly he lets his gaze travel to the bedroom window. Mercedes always told him that she was most at home in that room. The kitchen came second. The living room, third. Baxter always attributed her preference for the bedroom not merely to their intimacies there. It was for Mercedes a place of divestiture. It was the space where she dressed and undressed, where she preened, where she could examine her face or her body with the assurance of absolute privacy that such investigations required. Baxter sensed that she felt secure in that room. She trusted it to keep her (and their) secrets.

Staring at the bedroom window from the sidewalk, Baxter recalls the innumerable times that he and Mercedes had slept in that bedroom. He feels himself grow suddenly tired, remembering, but his mind is helpless before the onslaught of memory. He cannot forget that loving and making love were synonymous with Mercedes. She was never the dutiful wife who merely permitted or else barely tolerated sexual relations between the two of them. She yielded herself with a totality and passion that were beyond him. She made love not to him but with him in the sense that she created it between them when they touched one another or when her supple and quiet body became his twin. Their love-times together were never hurried, nor did she permit them to be interrupted by telephone calls or the like. She simply let the phone ring on such occasions, or else she removed the receiver from its cradle beforehand and placed it in a drawer of blouses or underwear to silence its buzzing or, after a time, the operator's repeated requests to hang up the phone. At those times she told Baxter that she thought the telephone was probably the rudest invention of all time. Blind and unignorably persistent, it could interrupt everything, she explained, from intimacy to death throes and somehow be absolved through the simple defense of ignorance.

Baxter shifts his gaze from the bedroom to the room that adjoins it. Another bedroom, it served both Mercedes and him as a sitting room where they could read together, open and sort and read their mail and then discuss whatever they had to discuss. It was furnished with padded leather chairs and a matching sofa, and there were end tables that Mercedes kept stacked with current periodicals as well as with dozens of newspapers, foreign and domestic, that Baxter received on a regular basis. At one point Mercedes decided that the two rooms should communicate with one another, and she had an archway built in the common wall between the two rooms. Often, after he had worked late and fallen asleep in his clothes, Baxter would waken to the smell of coffee in the house, and moments later Mercedes would appear in the sitting room with cups of hot coffee and assorted sweet rolls heated and enclosed in a cloth-napkin tent, and they would have breakfast together in the cool silence that they frequently shared in the morning. On such occasions Mercedes always let him awake gradually. She waited patiently for him to make his connections with the night before and then say whatever he wanted to say to her.

Baxter now sits down on his suitcase on the sidewalk. The act of walking to the front door and entering the house is something he feels incapable of doing. Perhaps if he distracts himself for a moment, he thinks, the courage will come. He looks up at the house again, and this time he focuses on the third-floor window. His darkroom and work-shop are there. He forces himself to think of photography and how he worked alone on his prints in the darkroom. It was work that consumed him with a sense of play and suffering at the same time. The clock did not exist for him then. Printing each photograph was like an experience in creating reality according to his own specifications. He remembers standing over the developing trays and watching the impressions gradually evolve into themselves on the paper submerged in swished fluids. He would shade and crop, darken and lighten, focus and refocus, repeat, repeat, repeat until he had the exact image that he had seen in his viewer when he made the photograph in the first place. Yet he was never satisfied. The final photograph was always off the mark. The camera always captured something that was either more or less than his eyes told him was there. The perfectly faithful photograph always eluded him, and yet he felt it was the one he would someday print. It was next, always next. He learned to live sullenly with the best he could do, but the feeling never left him that he could have done and would some day do better. After Mercedes was killed, his search for the perfect photograph became an obsession. He lived for nothing else but to take it and print it, particularly the one photograph that would show one human being facing some unspeakable horror as it was actually happening to him. It would be something like the look in a man's face when he stares back at a firing squad, but not quite. The horror would be there, but there would have to be surprise as well . . .

Baxter stands up and lifts the single piece of luggage that he has been sitting on. It contains only the camera equipment he managed to salvage from Lebanon. He begins to walk slowly toward the front door. The uneven stones under his soles have a rough familiarity about them. He is still stiff from the flight across the Atlantic. When he landed in New York, he explained the entire story of his "death" to the appropriate officials there but asked them to give him one day of grace before they contacted the press, and they reluctantly agreed. Now he is grateful for the respite.

He sets down his bag before the front door and reaches into his back pocket to make sure he still has the key to the house. He finds it tucked in a reserve compartment in his wallet where it has been for so long that it has a film of green mold on it. He pulls it free from the sticky leather. He is about to insert it in the keyhole when he notices that there is a light in the kitchen that he did not see from the sidewalk. Peering through the curtained door, he sees a woman sitting with her back to him at the kitchen table. He puts the key in the lock and opens the door.

"Tom?" the woman says, turning halfway in the chair.

"Who are you?" asks Baxter.

Louise stands up quickly, knocking over the chair as Baxter moves across the hall and into the kitchen. She suddenly drops the cup she is holding and leans back against the table as if she has lost or is about to lose her balance.

"Who are you?" Baxter repeats. "What are you doing in my house?"

THE BOY'S MOTHER WILL ADDRESS THE BOY as George Albert Daniel while they are standing near the ticket counter and will explain to him, as will the ticket clerks, that he can keep his dog with him for another half an hour only. After that, they explain, the dog will have to be loaded in the cargo hold with the luggage. The boy will listen to everything that is being said to him but will continue to clutch the plastic crate that holds the dog. The dog, a dachshund, will remain immobile in the crate, which is ventilated at both ends with mesh-screened windows. Perhaps by choice, perhaps by accident, the boy will be holding the crate in such a way that the dachshund's rear end will be facing the adults in front of him.

After five minutes of fruitless negotiation with the boy, the mother will tell the clerks that she will have to speak to George Albert Daniel alone. She will lead the boy away from the ticket counter and under the arch that leads into the interior of the TWA terminal. They will pass a short man who is holding a trombone case. The trombone case will distract the boy, and he will put down the crated dog in front of the man and smile up at him. The man will put the trombone case behind him, and the boy's mother will say emphatically, "George Albert Daniel, come here," and the dog will bark twice. The man with the trombone case will move to the other side of the arch.

Once they are near the large window at the rear of the terminal, the boy and his mother will locate two seats beside two Franciscan nuns. The boy will sit between one of the nuns and his mother and hold the crated dog with both hands on his lap. The mother will begin explaining all over, this time calling him Georgie instead of George Albert Daniel, that the dog cannot travel with him in the passenger section. She will tell him with a forced smile that they will all be together again when the plane lands in Chicago. The boy's only response will be to hold the crate more tightly.

When the shooting begins, the boy will watch people starting to run past him, but he will remain seated. He will hear the Franciscan nun at his side scream. He will see his mother topple backward with a bullet in her shoulder. She will be a year recovering, and she will never be able to raise

her arm above her head again. The dog will be killed immediately, but it will be the crate's and the dog's blunting of
the bullet's force that will save the boy's life. For years the
boy will remember the wet heat of the dog's blood on his
knees.

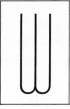

HEN SHE WAS IN HER TWENTIES, Louise made daily entries in a diary. She found that holding herself to account every night for the events of the day helped her to understand herself, and the self-knowledge she gained gave her a certain confidence as well as a certain peace. Later she changed from written entries to using a tape recorder. Just before she went to bed, she would turn on the recorder and think out loud, and on the following morning, while she ate her breakfast, she would rewind the tape and listen to herself.

Baxter's return from Lebanon was such a surprise to her that she was drawn to tape her thoughts about it in order to understand the change it brought to her life. As long as she thought of him as dead, she dealt with him as a finished story, a subject for research. Alive, he became a presence she had to brace herself to confront.

Listening to her tape recordings helped Louise regain her self-possession, but never permanently. Each time she saw Baxter, she had to start all over again.

One morning, weeks after his return, she rewinds the tape to the very beginning and listens to it from start to finish.

"At first I didn't believe my eyes. I didn't know what to say or how to react to a man I thought was already dead. I'd thought of him as dead for months. When he walked into the kitchen, I dropped the cup of coffee I was holding. I just couldn't hold it. I felt I was seeing a real resurrection. Down deep I had never really accepted his death, I suppose. Reading his letters and listening to his voice on the tape and spending all that time in his house and studying those photographs made me think of him as alive. But *thinking* of him as alive and then seeing him there in the kitchen are two different things, let me tell you. Just as I was ready to call it a night, there he was. Even if I was prepared for it, I would have been shaken. But who can be prepared for something like that?

"After I told him who I was and why I was there and explained everything about Tom and the program and all the rest of it, he still looked at me as an intruder. And that's been the way he's looked at me for weeks now. I see him almost every day, and there's no change. It took a lot of persuading on Tom's part to convince him to go ahead with the program. Tom just told him that all the material was in place, and what was wrong with finishing what we'd already started? Tom even showed him what we'd done, and I followed up by telling him that the whole program would be a series of stills in motion interspersed with commentary. Well, he listened, but I could tell that he didn't like my approach. He didn't say two words though. He gave me the impression that he resented what he knew I'd learned about him. That much was quite clear. If there's one thing I've learned in the past few weeks, it's that Bede Diogenes Baxter is one private man. Each day I saw him I realized that he was everything I thought he would be, but I could never get close to him. He kept me at a distance. He kept everyone at a distance. But what I'd learned about him gave me a certain advantage over everybody else, and he detected that, and he didn't appreciate it. But still I was almost hypnotized by him. All that I'd learned about him and all that I was still learning about him every day monopolized my thoughts. Thinking about any other thing was an interruption. I couldn't spend enough time around him.

"But he preferred Tom. Tom was the one he talked to. Early on, it was Tom who dealt with the newspapers and the television people. There were reporters and television crews all over the place. Everyone wanted to know what *really* happened to him in Lebanon. They wanted all the details. But Bax just told them so much and that was it. After a week went by, the story was old news, and we could get back to work. But Tom was the one who kept everything from turning into a circus.

"Afterward I kept noticing how Bax went out of his way

not to be alone with me or not be in places where we would somehow be left alone together because that would mean that we would have to talk to one another. He wasn't ready for that. He let me know that he didn't want any part of me until one Sunday night—it was just a week ago—he telephoned me and said in two or three serious, prethought sentences that he wanted to apologize for his behavior toward me. When I tried to make light of it, he said his manner had nothing to do with me. It was something that was very difficult for him to explain, but he finally told me that I had touched a part of his life that was reserved for only two people. He knew I was only doing my job. Then he said that he hoped we could work together from that time on without any problem. I thought that I should respond, but I couldn't think of a word. He ended by telling me he appreciated my accepting his apology even though it was a bit late. Then we said good-bye, and that was that.

"The next day all the uneasiness and the suspicion were gone, as if they never existed in the first place. We just became two people with a job ahead of us, and we wanted to do the best job we could. We worked together so well that I couldn't believe it, as if we'd been rehearsing all our lives to do just what we were doing. We became perfectionists. And Bax became the man I had come to know from his tapes and from his letters, and, to tell the truth, I couldn't have been happier. In fact, I can't remember having been happier in my life.

"In the midst of all that, he kept one side of himself under lock and key. Last night we drove home together. It wasn't a long drive. Just ten minutes. I asked him if it was hard being in his house by himself. I didn't mean anything by it. It was just what I was thinking at the time. He turned and looked at me with a smile that wasn't a smile. Instead of answering me, he asked me if I liked Duke Ellington's music. Before I could respond, he proceeded to talk about Duke Ellington as if we'd been talking about Duke Ellington all evening. That was just his way of letting me know that he didn't want to talk about things he didn't want to talk about.

"Of course, what I couldn't tell him was that I'd fallen for him. In fact, I'd fallen for him for months before he came back from Lebanon. The notebooks and the letters and the tape recording took care of that. I learned to love a man with the courage of his tastes and his skills and who was not afraid to face the real pain in the real faces of this world. And he photographed it not as an exploiter but just as a witness. All the pictures of his that I saw made me feel that I'd been missing the real point of everything all my life and that the real point was in his pictures. They showed me that the man who took them was a man who still had what used to be called a heart. That doesn't mean much anymore, but it means a lot to me because that's the one thing you either have or don't have, and if you have it, you're absolutely special. To date I've met no men (apart from Tom and Bax) and damned few women who have it, but I know it when I'm in the presence of it. It's not something that I have myself. I think about things too much. I don't just respond on instinct. So maybe I'm especially sensitive to what I don't have myself, but with Bax it's there. The photographs prove it's there.

"I never felt anything like this for Harry. I was even starting to think that feelings like this were just an illusion.

Every time I have lunch with Brenda from Circulation, she's ready to tell me that I'm still a dreamer. She's been divorced for three years, and she said she wouldn't get married again on a bet. 'Why should I give up my freedom to be with some man? I don't need that. I can earn my own living. So why do I need a man to complicate my life?' Then I say, 'Brenda, you're just a cynic. Don't you believe in love anymore?' And she gives me that look of hers and says, 'Louise, I believed in love once. That was enough. But that doesn't mean that I've given up my sexual life. It's just like eating. That's the way I look at it. You have to eat when you're hungry, don't you? That's all that love is for me. You satisfy yourself with some man who wants to satisfy himself. So who's hurt? You're both consenting adults, aren't you? Everybody makes such a deal out of sex. It's not much different than shaking hands, really. There's one man I go out with, and we actually take care of one another in advance so that we can go out to dinner or the theater and just face and enjoy the evening for what it is and not be expecting the big thrill afterward. Honest, Louise, it's much better that way. You should try it. It's almost like hygiene. If I'm not satisfied when I need to be satisfied, I get cranky and I get these damned migraines that drive me out of my mind. It's just good therapy. That's all that sex is.' I don't know if she really believes that, but she sounds as if she does. All I know is that I can't live like that. It reminds me too much of how I was living with Harry. We shared the same apartment, and I'd listen to what he said to me, and we did some things together, and three times a week like clockwork our organs would find one another. Love has to be more than that. I kept wanting to give myself and not just a part of me, and I tried to do that with Harry until I realized that I couldn't. I just thank God there were no children. Harry took care of that. He just didn't want children, not right away. He said he needed time to establish himself in the sportswear business, so he would use a condom or at the last minute he would pull away from me and let it happen right there on the sheet or somewhere on the bed. I kept telling myself that he would change, but it never happened.

"Maybe it's because of Harry that Bax seems like such an exception to me. He's just different. I really have to concentrate on what I'm doing when I'm on the job with him, or my mind goes off every which way. That's the effect he has on me. I feel like a high school girl around him. Sometimes I want to blurt right out what I feel about him, but I can't bring myself to do it. What if he laughed at me? I think I'd die if he laughed at me. He must see that I care for him. He must see that when I look at him. But he never says anything, never shows anything, never lets anything distract us from the job we're doing.

"I envy what he feels for his wife, what he still feels for her. I could see in every one of his photographs of her that she was a woman who was really loved. Even in the sad pictures, she looked like a happy woman. She saw a side of Bax he never lets me see. If I had one wish, I'd wish more than anything that I could be to him for five minutes what she was to him. I wish I could know that someone could look at me, all of me, just once the way he must have looked at her. That would be enough for me.

"Now my life is just my job. I don't know Wednesday from Friday anymore. The weekends are the hardest times because I don't have to go to work, and I have to wait until Monday again to lose myself in what I'm doing.

"I keep thinking of those terrible nights when I wake up

in the middle of darkness, and I feel absolutely alone. I just
lie there, listening. Or sometimes I turn on the light and
read until my eyes get tired. But I keep thinking what it
must be like to sleep beside someone you really love, to
share the night with him that way. It makes me think that
lovers are like two sailors on the small boat of a double bed
that's at sea in the middle of time and space. And they
embrace one another or they sleep side by side in the midst
of that sea, and they're the center of the only world that
matters. And then I think of Bax and me like that.

"Facts are facts. I don't know if he even thinks about me
that way. And I say to myself, 'Face the facts, Louise, and
stop dreaming. You're thinking like a coed. You're thinking with your hips. Snap out of it. That's the way you
thought about Harry before you saw Harry for what he was
and what he still is and what he'll always be. You just didn't
see him that way until it was too late, and then you closed
your eyes to it. As long as your eyes were closed, it was all
right. But eventually you had to open your eyes. You can't
kid yourself forever. And you realize that you can't love
what you think you saw in somebody else if it's not there
and never was there.'

"I'm not going to pretend anymore. I'm not going to
torture myself with what my life could have been. Tomorrow I'll be with Bax again, and sure as the sun I'll fall for
him all over again. Maybe he'll notice that. Maybe things
will change."

THE DAILY DANGERS THAT BAXTER FACED in Lebanon had done much to exorcise desire in him. Living under or in the midst of artillery duels or crossfire, aware that a sniper's shot could occur at any moment in which any target was fair game, convinced that human life in such circumstances meant less to the combatants than the lives of mice or flies, Baxter felt a deadening at the core of his personality that human beings eventually feel when absurdity and only absurdity separates the quick and the dead.

There was only the exquisite pleasure of the next breath that was valuable to him, and on some days even that prospect lost its allure. For more than two months in Lebanon he lived only for the next day, hoping secretly for the lethal rendezvous that he was convinced awaited him there but denying it all the same every time he thought of it.

For months and even years after Mercedes was killed, he felt he was living posthumously. Yet it was not entirely posthumous. Something in him died with her, to be sure, but what remained alive would not abide by the rules of what death had done to him. His desires and appetites remained as they were, however latent, and yet even to think of involving or indulging himself with another woman reawakened those lineaments of his love for Mercedes that any possible involvement or indulgence seemed to defile. His love for Mercedes had once and for all fused affection and desire within him. And they remained inseparable even after her death. The result then was that love awakened latent desires that he could never completely ignore. They intensified or diminished, depending on his moods.

After two years he allowed himself to be accessible—not the personal self that had lived and been entombed with Mercedes but his ongoing self, which he tended to regard as someone apart from his real personality. This was the self he fed, shaved, washed, dressed and tended to. It was the self that he permitted an occasional dalliance or indulgence, but he treated such indulgences afterward with a cynicism and even a scorn that never permitted their reoccurrence and never allowed them to become personal.

It took him months to realize that his formula of work

and itinerant pleasure now and then was not working for him. His world went on according to its own timetable, but he felt himself slipping into arrears. This bothered him, but it did not bother him enough to change. He simply resigned himself to it as his fate. He saw himself as a man in the act of sinking, and something in him wanted him to sink quietly, painlessly, even nobly. It was when he was in this frame of mind that he would search out those parts of the world where danger of sudden death was a constant possibility, and he would go there, camera in hand. He did not go with the calculation of a strategist, but with the impulsive decisiveness of a man who chooses, for reasons he cannot understand, to dive through utter darkness into deep, cold water—the decision being a combination of daring, whim, fear, conviction and, simultaneously, regret.

When he reached the conclusion that his life in the United States was more predictable than his life in Lebanon might be, he departed for Lebanon. But still his sense of living a posthumous life did not change. In fact, it only grew stronger. And it was this feeling more than any other that tended to deaden all his feelings for other people as well as toward himself. Food was simply food. He ate because he had to. From time to time, he tried to go without food as long as possible. He hated to have to deal with his hungers, hated the fact that he had to relieve his bladder or his bowels, hated to have to deal with his body's recurring necessities. As the days passed in Lebanon, he felt that he was keeping a corpse alive. And this made him look at everyone else as another corpse. The women whom he saw every day had no effect upon him, no capacity to arouse him, no appeal. He simply looked on them as females of the species. Finally he saw that this lack of appetite for life in all its forms and the death he passively desired were converting his life into boredom.

When he returned to the United States, he let his former sense of life take possession of him little by little, day by day. With Tom's help he dealt with the press tactfully but undramatically until the reporters came to regard him and his return from Lebanon as a story not worth pursuing. This enabled him to concentrate on those rolls of film that he had salvaged from Lebanon and to print them as he wanted. He studied each of the negatives microscopically, hoping that somewhere in the lot he had taken the photograph he wanted to take. He felt certain that, in a country where horror was as common as breathing, he had managed to take the one prophetic photograph that would be his warning to the world, but he never found it.

It was Louise's presence that disturbed him most. She appeared to know secrets about him that hovered like a tacit form of unadmitted knowledge between them when they were in each other's presence. She never divulged anything, but he resented her having a certain advantage over him as a result of her research. He was always waiting for her to ask him a question that would infringe on that part of his life he kept to himself. For that reason he took pains to make sure they were never alone together, even when they were working on the program. As long as he could keep their relationship strictly professional, he could deal with her matter-of-factly. He did not know how he would converse with her on personal matters, and he did not want to have to find out.

From the first day of their working together, Louise had

suggested that he call her Louise. He accepted that, but he did not reciprocate. The result was that she addressed him as Mr. Baxter, and he seemed comfortable with that.

Baxter could not help but be impressed with her on the job. She was always prepared, always in complete possession of herself, always ready with the right suggestion at the right time. There was no question in his mind that she wanted the program to show him at his best, but he did not know if she wanted this for professional reasons or for reasons that were only hers to know. He continued to be puzzled by that. And the fact that he was puzzled compelled him to concentrate on her when he had no other reason to do so. Often he found himself looking at her when she was busy with the crew or with Tom. He not only looked at her face; he looked at her totally. He found himself memorizing her way of walking, and he liked the knack she had of putting her hair in order merely by shaking her head.

Alone once at lunch with Tom, Baxter asked, "This girl Louise, Tom. What's her background?"

"College graduate. Small college in central Pennsylvania. She was in this business before, and then she married. She was married to a sporting-goods salesman."

"Was?"

"Yes, was. I think they're separated for keeps now. She's been back with me for more than a year. Worked her way up. She's a terrific worker. She was the only one I thought of for this job on you."

"I can see she's good, Tom."

"Is there a problem?"

"No, no, not a problem between us, if that's what you mean. It's just a little disconcerting to work with somebody who seems to know more about you than you know about yourself."

"That's what makes her indispensable, Bax. But you have to remember that she was working on this before you came back. She did a lot of research. You were just a name to her before that. But she stayed with it, day and night, until your whole life was second nature to her."

"What happened to her marriage?"

"I don't know the inside facts, but from what I saw, it was a case of totally different personalities, totally different ideas of what was important. I've met Harry a few times. That's her husband, her ex-husband. He's Babbitt in running shoes."

"Any children?"

"No."

"What's she doing with her life now?"

"Living like a straight single from what I see." Pausing, Tom looked at Baxter and smiled. "Are you interested, Bax?" He waited, but Baxter continued to eat his ham sandwich. "She'd be good for you, Bax. I'm telling you that not just as a friend but as Mercedes' brother."

"Not interested, Tom. My camera's the only wife I want for the moment and from now on."

Tom could see from the set expression on Baxter's face that this was a subject Baxter did not want Tom to pursue.

"Well," said Tom. "How do you like the show so far?"

"From what I've seen—fine. But I'm no judge. You really shouldn't expect an objective answer from me, Tom. In fact, I'm the last one you should ask. Put me behind my own camera, and I know what I'm talking about. But commenting on a television show about myself—what can I say?"

"But is there anything that we're leaving out, or is there anything that we're not stressing enough?"

"Only that I haven't taken *the* picture, the *one* picture I want to take."

"Can you describe it? Maybe we can include a segment where you can describe it, where *you're* the camera."

"I can't in so many words, Tom. All I can talk about is the feeling I want people to have when they look at it." He paused and thought of what he had just said. "There's a statement for you. If I said that on television, they'd think I was crazy, wouldn't they? I want people to get a certain feeling from a picture I've yet to take. That doesn't even make sense to me."

"Come on, Bax, you can be more specific than that."

"I really can't, Tom. All I can tell you is that it's the kind of picture for me to take at this time in my life. And the fact is that I may never take it because it's something that just has to happen. It's a mix of chance, luck, timing and, of course, me." He stopped and looked at Tom to see if he understood, or at least sympathized, with what he was trying to say. And in that brief look he saw an older Tom. His brown hair was thinning, and some of the hair ends were flecked with gray. He wore glasses permanently now—black horn-rims with the bifocal division clearly evident. The nose he had broken when he was a minor-league catcher and which had never healed straight disguised his essential thoughtfulness and generosity and made him look like an ex-boxer who could turn pugnacious in a minute in what was a highly competitive business. It was still Tom that Baxter saw, but he also saw for the first time what the years had done to him. As he watched, he could tell that Tom, like the born listener he was, was making a serious effort to understand him. "Here," continued Bax, "let me explain it another way. Let me tell you what I came away with in Lebanon. Now remember, this is a country that is like a lot of other countries in this world. It has a lot of natural beauty. It has a cosmopolitan society, at least in the major cities. It has a significant place in the world of commerce. Perhaps I should say that it *had* a lot of these qualities before it began to come apart at the seams, first slowly, then in a lot of different places, then everywhere. It turns into a country that is ruled by the gun. It's invaded by countries that have designs on it, different designs, but still designs, and these are countries that play for high stakes and couldn't care less about the Lebanese people and how many they have to get rid of if they get in the way. And so you have invasion imposed on anarchy. You have Lebanese killing Lebanese. You have Syrians killing Lebanese. You have Israelis killing Lebanese when they marched on Beirut—something over twenty thousand. The population forgets its own so-called government and breaks down into tribes, and the tribes are armed to the teeth. You have a lot of anonymous murder by car bombs, plastique, grenades, all the rest. It's war. It's not the kind of war we have a vocabulary for yet, but it's war. And it brings out the best and the worst in people. There are doctors there who keep on operating while the bullets fly. I've seen men captured and executed with their hands tied behind them with their own intestines. And I've seen girls raped so many times that they've lost their minds. It's like the return of Genghis Khan. And yet you have to remember that Lebanon is a modern country, a sophisticated country. What's happening there now would have been unthinkable fifteen years ago."

"I still don't get the connection between Lebanon and the picture you want to take," said Tom, frowning.

"Do you remember that picture I showed you, Tom? Bob Capa's picture?"

"The one of the soldier in Spain being shot?"

"Yes, that one. Capa clicked the shutter just as the man was taking the bullet."

"I remember it."

"Well, there was no way for Capa to know he was going to take a picture like that. In fact, to this day I don't know how in the hell he took it, but he did, and the proof is there in black and white. If you study that picture, you can learn as much about that kind of war as there is to learn. It's all there—a man being hit by someone from such a distance that the hit was probably accidental. The man just happened to be in the way, in the line of fire. And the rest of the war in Spain and the war in Europe that followed it was prefigured in that photograph. People were killed at long distance by rifle, by machine gun, by howitzer, by dive bomber, by Flying Fortress, by whatever. And Capa prophesied it all with one photograph." He paused to make sure that Tom was abreast of him. "What I'd give anything to do, Tom, is to be able to take a photograph that would show people the kind of future we're probably going to have to face. I don't mean it's the only future for everybody, but I think it's a likely one. I said all this, if you remember, on the tape I left you before I went to Lebanon."

"Tell me again, Bax. It's been months since I heard it."

"All right, look at the possibilities. The first possibility is nuclear war. Nobody wants that because nobody would survive it. There's even a slogan about it. 'No victors, just victims.' The second possibility is a localized war that is nonnuclear. Iran and Iraq. That business between Argentina and the Brits in the Falklands. Grenada, if you want to stretch a point. They can be short or prolonged, but the weapons stay conventional. The third possibility and the most likely is a repetition *outside* of Lebanon of what is happening *in* Lebanon. It can happen anywhere at any time."

"How?"

"All it takes is one man with the knowledge of explosives, even nuclear explosives, and the means to deliver them, even if he has to sacrifice himself to deliver them. That's the war I'm talking about, Tom. And there's not much of a defense against it. It can happen in front of an apartment building or in a terminal or in the middle of a stadium during a game. What kind of a defense can be mounted against a single man who is willing to give up his life to make sure that he hits the target, particularly if you don't know who he is or what the target is or when he's going to make his move? There's none. Remember that truck driver who killed all those Marines at Khalde? There's a perfect example. Take that kind of mentality and export it, and you can have Lebanon all over the place. It's here. It's there. It's just under your skin. It sounds like a Hollywood script, but a one-man war is with us from now on. A real possibility. And the weapons could be nuclear or conventional."

"It does sound like a Hollywood script, Bax."

"Maybe it does, Tom, but there are a lot of men in the eastern Mediterranean who have a ton of grievances, personal and political, in their guts and who have nothing to lose. And we're not their favorite country at the moment. We have a habit of being on the wrong side of justice over there, and we're paying for it, and we'll continue to pay for it. Think about it for a minute. Except for the past ten years or so, were Americans at risk in that part of the world? Hell no they weren't. But now look. Just look."

"But I still want to know what all that has to do with the picture you're dying to take."

"Remember Capa's picture? That picture was a prophecy. Those who looked at it at the time didn't realize that it was, but it was. And later on in the war I saw a photograph in *Life*'s archives of two Hungarian secret policemen who had done some dirty work for the Nazis or the Russians and who were brought to trial. It was really a street trial, and they were condemned to death on the spot, according to the transcript. I remember two photographs of them. One shows them standing together. They look calm. One of them is even smiling. The next photograph was taken an instant later. They are both flinching in this one. They both have their hands up like this in front of their faces to ward off the bullets of the firing squad. The photograph shows them at just that second. I regard that photograph as a prophecy. It tells you everything you have to know about what awaits traitors when the tables are turned." He cleared his throat and sipped water from his glass. "Now just suppose, Tom, that I was lucky enough to be somewhere in Europe or even here in the States or maybe back in Lebanon when some kamikaze was just about to go into his act. If I could take a picture of that and survive to develop it and print it, that would be my prophecy. That would state in a single black-and-white still everything I've been trying to explain to you for the past ten minutes or so. And it couldn't be refuted or denied. The photograph would convince your eyes. It would be like a warning. Anybody who looked at it would have to pause. You know what it's like when you hear a speeding driver suddenly hit the brakes. You don't see the car. You just hear the speed, and then you hear the brakes. And the brakes are screeching like hysteria. Later you might hear the collision or the crunch, but for a moment there is only the sound of brakes. And all the time you're listening. You're holding your breath. You have to hold your breath whether you want to or not. I want to take a photograph that will make people hold their breath, Tom." He paused and repeated softly. "I want the picture to make them hold their breath."

IT'S COME DOWN TO the last two photographs. Each of them has been enlarged and mounted on separate display tables, and there is a single stool posted equidistantly between them. Baxter is examining each of the photographs carefully while Louise stands several yards behind him. Her plan is for Baxter to be seated on the stool and to discuss each of the photographs as the program closes.

"These have lost a lot of definition by enlarging them,

but I suppose that's the price you have to pay," says Baxter, squinting at one section of one of the photographs.

"We did the best we could. The main thing is that I want them flanking you while you speak. The only other alternative would be to zoom in on a smaller, clearer reproduction of each photograph and then dissolve to you. That might be better photographically, but it's not the effect I want for the ending."

Baxter walks to the second photograph and peruses it with a jeweler's eye. He reminds Louise of an artist examining the surface of a painting or of a surgeon studying an X-ray. She watches him shake his head no from time to time.

"A lot of subtlety's been lost, Louise," says Baxter.

"I'm sorry, Mr. Baxter. That just couldn't be helped," explains Louise.

"I know, I know," answers Baxter, resigned to the fact.

"When the audience looks at the . . ." Louise begins.

"Maybe that's the problem," interrupts Baxter.

"What's the problem?"

"*Looking.* You really don't *look* at a photograph. You *read* a photograph. Sometimes you read it in Chinese, up and down or down and up. Sometimes in Arabic, from right to left the way you read Picasso's *Guernica.* If you read a photograph the wrong way, you can miss everything."

"But how many people in the audience are sophisticated enough to understand that?" asks Louise.

"Not many," Baxter says dismissively. "That's the problem. Most people don't know how to look. Or rather they look, but they don't see."

Louise moves in on the first photograph. Taking Baxter's

cue, she starts to read the photograph from one side to the other, then from the bottom up. In both cases she feels nothing. Then she starts from the top down, and the photograph suddenly comes alive for her. She feels herself being drawn into it, as if she is actually there.

Beginning again from the top of the photograph to the bottom, Louise sees first a noon sky above the roofs of two stores and an intervening house. Even in black and white the sky shines as the brightest part of the photograph. Flowing toward her like a stream between the facades of the two stores is a street. The street is unpaved. It is muddy as if from a recent rain. There is a cairn of watermelons in front of one of the stores. In front of the other are two white chickens tethered to separate stakes. In the upper center of the photograph there is a large puddle. It punctuates the middle of the rain-saturated street. Studying it, Louise understands why Baxter cropped the photograph as he did. Her eyes pass automatically to a smaller puddle just below it. This is the center of the picture. On her back and slightly to the right of the puddle is a woman, or what seems to be a woman. The fact that she is slightly off center disrupts the symmetry of the entire picture. Louise's eyes keep returning to her, and this, she realizes, is exactly what Baxter intended. The puddle muck conceals the bottom half of the woman's body, and her ankle-length dress is water-heavy on her legs. She is barefooted, and her left foot is twisted unnaturally so that it is flat with the muddy street. The woman's arms are extended in a mock crucifixion. Her face is covered with part of her head scarf.

The casual horror of the photograph chills Louise. Then she looks to the right side of the photograph. Standing side

by side in front of the watermelon pile are three children—
two boys and a girl. Louise can tell it is a girl because she
is wearing a biblike dress that does not cover the lower half
of her body. She is sucking her thumb and looking at the
woman's corpse, but the expression on her face indicates
that she does not know what a corpse is. The boy beside her
is holding her hand, and he is smiling. Of all the things that
will remain with Louise from this photograph, none will
eclipse that incongruous smile. The other boy is slightly
older, and he is holding an automatic weapon in his right
hand with the butt resting on his right hip. He seems deadly
serious.

"Where was this photograph taken?" asks Louise.

"Somewhere in the Chouf. I don't remember."

"Was it difficult for you to take a picture like this?"

Baxter looks at her quizzically. "Do you mean photographically?"

"No," says Louise. "I mean just taking the picture, that
kind of a picture."

"You get used to it."

"I don't think I could."

"Well, you're not a photographer."

"All right, I'm not a photographer, but what difference
does that make?"

"It makes *all* the difference."

"I'm afraid I have a little trouble understanding that, Mr.
Baxter."

"So do I."

"But you take the pictures anyway?"

"Right."

Louise turns to the second photograph. She tries reading

it from side to side and then from top to bottom and from bottom to top. Finally, she studies it from the center out, and the photograph turns instantly real. The photograph is like a cameo. Centered within the cameo is a woman of perhaps seventy years of age. She is squatting beside a mound-grave on which there is a sprig of white wildflowers in a half-filled drinking glass. The woman's copious black skirt tents her legs and ankles as she squats, and she is extending her hands palms-upward like a beggar waiting for baksheesh.

"Do you know what that woman is doing?" asks Baxter.

"She looks like she's begging."

"No, she's praying. Look at her eyes."

Louise studies the upturned eyes and nods. The woman's face is sculpted by a lifetime of pain, and her expression is of someone who has no tears left to shed but who is still weeping. The grave in front of her is obviously the reason for her grief. There is a small, flat rock serving as the grave's marker, and pasted on the flat side of the rock-marker is a photograph of a dark-haired young man, a boy really, with his first moustache. He is smiling. The boy's smile and the old woman's anguish parenthesize the whole photograph for Louise. They counterpoint one another—the boy's mustachioed smile, the beginning of manhood, the innocent but complete confidence and, on the other hand, the etched pain in the woman's face, especially around the pinched slits that are her eyes. The woman's white hair is tied with a bandana that was once white, and she has small rings in either earlobe. Louise notices that there is very little light in the photograph. What light there is is not the dimming light of evening but the sudden lightlessness that appears when a bank of dark clouds comes between the sun and the earth.

"Was this picture taken at the same time as the first one?" she asks.

"Actually it was taken first. By almost half a year."

"In the same place?"

"No. This was in a refugee camp near Tyre. That's south of Beirut. The boy in the photograph is a Palestinian, and the old woman is his grandmother. He was killed in an Israeli air strike. It happens all the time."

"That's the one thing about photography I could never understand, Mr. Baxter."

"What's that?"

"Taking a photograph of someone who is suffering while it's happening, and you see it, and you take the picture regardless."

"It's a consideration but not a photographic one. Just look at *that* picture from the point of view of composition. It's an ideal picture. Very little movement. You just wait for the right moment, and the camera does the rest of the work."

"But doesn't something inside of you want to help?"

"Well," says Baxter, looking away from her. He is remembering how Mercedes had repeatedly asked him the same question. "There is something like that. There always is. But you have to resist it so you can function as a photographer. You have to be a little like an officer in the army. You do what has to be done, and you try not to think of casualties. It's something like that with me. If you enter into every subject personally, then you simply can't do your job. Nothing would be done at all, or you would end up with just a lot of pleasant pictures. And I think you would agree that there's a lot about life that isn't pleasant. So when you take a photograph of something that is unpleasant or unsettling, like that grandmother in that photograph, you have to make a decision about who you are at that moment—a photographer or someone else."

"But how can you divide yourself in two like that? If everybody is a human being, a person, how can anybody do anything without being personal about it? You just can't retreat into your job and think you've solved the problem."

"You have to. If everybody thought your way, there would be no photojournalism at all. If you stop to console an old woman at the grave of her grandson and not take a photograph of her, it might do her some good. I agree with that. But if you capture her grief on film so that other people will see it, then you can touch the emotions of hundreds or thousands of other people."

"So the end justifies the means. That's an old rationalization, Mr. Baxter."

"It's the best I can offer. For a man like me it makes photography possible."

"It makes *impersonality* possible." Louise pauses. She can see that the conversation is on the verge of becoming an argument, and she does not want that. "I'm sorry, Mr. Baxter. I'm asking too many questions. I'm sure you've thought through all this much more thoroughly than I. I was just thinking out loud."

"Those questions come up from time to time. I've thought about them. I still think about them."

Louise turns back to examine the second photograph and scrutinizes the face of the old woman beside the grave. She concentrates on it until it hurts her to look at it any longer.

"What I'd like to know if I were a photographer is whether I could take a picture like that if that were _my_ mother or _my_ grandmother there." She faces Baxter and asks, "If that were your mother in that street, could you have taken that picture?"

"But it wasn't my mother."

"But suppose it was?"

"I don't deal in supposes."

"Well, I don't have any illusions about it. If that were my mother, I wouldn't be thinking about photography at all. I'd be right there on the ground beside her."

Reminded of a problem he had discussed often with Mercedes, Baxter remains silent. He sees that he is no closer to a solution now than he was then.

"What happened to her?" asks Louise.

"Who?"

"The woman in the picture."

"No idea. I took the picture and left."

"I don't think I could have done that."

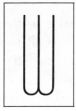

WHEN LOUISE RETURNS TO HER APARTMENT, she is still disturbed with how Baxter answered her questions. She did not expect him to be so matter-of-fact. It was as if each answer was another brick in the wall that he was deliberately building between them.

Later, while lying in bed, she speaks into her tape recorder.

"All these weeks and so far I have yet to see a sign of what I saw in him when I was listening to him talk on the tapes or when I was looking at his photographs. No sign at all of that other Baxter. Every time I talk to him I might as well be talking to a carpenter about carpentry. There's not a hint of heart in him.

"Maybe I was wrong from the start about him. Maybe I'm just reading into him what I thought was there. Or do I really mean what I *want* to be there? I suppose the truth is that he's really no different from all the other men I've met to date, just more secretive, that's all. I don't know. There's such a deliberate sadness about him all the time, and I know that it's probably because he lost his wife the way he did. Sometimes I think he acts as if he has to be sad the way Mother acted after Dad died. It was as if she had to suffer. She thought she had to keep a definite sad side to her life as a tribute to the life that she and Dad had together. Once I asked her why, and she just said I couldn't understand. She said nobody could understand. And then I said that Dad would be the last one to want her to be sad, but she would just shake her head and keep saying I couldn't understand, and then she'd cry, and I'd feel terrible for having said what I said. Maybe I don't understand and maybe the loneliness makes the survivors act the way they do, but in my book it certainly doesn't do justice to the dead. You can't share in their dying by being sad all the time. And what good does it do anyway except to make the person still left alive more depressed than he has a right to be. And what can it mean to the dead, one way or the other?

"Baxter has the same tendency that I saw in Mother. The only one who can make him forget it for a few minutes is Tom. Baxter's just himself around Tom. He just turns into a human being despite himself. But when he's with me, the wall goes up, and we stick to job talk. He won't let me get one foot or even one inch inside of his private side. He has the keys to his own cathedral, and he keeps it locked to everyone but Tom. And Tom doesn't probe. He just listens. I think he really respects Baxter's wish to stay inside of himself for as long as he wants.

"Who am I to go barging into Baxter's life? I don't have any rights to do that. I'm just a co-worker. He doesn't vary from that when we're together. I guess in one sense I should be grateful. It doesn't complicate the job. It's what I feel that's complicating the job. I'm the one who wants a romantic side to be there, not him. So the problem's with me, not with him. He's just being who he is, and I don't have a right in the world to expect any more than that. Besides, he's older than I am. Sixteen years older is a lot of years older, isn't it? But then again I've known a lot of women who were younger than their husbands, sometimes by a decade or more. But what's the big difference if they love one another?

"Harry and I were born almost on the same day of the same year, and what good did it do us? Whatever love is, it sure doesn't have much to do with age. It's what you feel for one another, isn't it? I tried to feel something for Harry, but it wasn't there. And all I did feel was guilt for marrying him. But that's over now. It disappeared when Harry took me to his apartment and had what Brenda would call a quick lay. That's all I was to Harry—just a quick lay. And there he was, telling me about the new love in his life as if I should feel flattered. I keep asking myself why I let him have me that night. I don't know if I wanted him or if I was just falling back into an old habit."

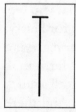

OM IS ABOUT TO LEAVE BAXTER'S KITCHEN, where he and Baxter have been discussing whether the program should run for thirty or sixty minutes.

"So we'll go for sixty," says Tom. "We have more than enough material."

"Whatever you say," answers Baxter.

"You don't sound very enthusiastic."

Baxter smiles and puts his hand on Tom's shoulder. "I've lost a lot of my enthusiasm. I've lost my taste for it the way

I've lost my taste for cigars. On that tape I left for you I spent a lot of time talking about politics and aesthetics and some other things, but they all seem superficial to me now. I used to eat politics, remember?"

"Sure, I remember."

"Now it bores me to death. And talking about anything bores me to death, even talking about photography. I've lost whatever it was that made me enthusiastic. So if I give you the impression that I'm not enthusiastic about the program, I'm just being consistent. But I won't stand in your way. I'll do whatever you want me to do."

"Thanks, Bax. You won't be sorry."

Together they walk to the front door. Just as Tom is about to leave, he faces Baxter and says, "You know you're welcome at our house anytime. Linda and I both want you to know that. You don't even have to call. Just come over."

"Thanks, Tom. I appreciate it. I'll take you up on it."

"Good night, Bax."

"Good night, Tom."

Baxter closes the front door behind Tom and trudges slowly up the stairs to his darkroom on the third floor. Before Tom arrived, he'd been developing the last of the rolls of film that he had brought back from Lebanon. Returning now to his darkroom is like returning to Beirut and the Chouf and the southern tip of the Bekaa, and his mood is of a man returning to an underworld. He showed some of the finished prints to Tom and asked if he wanted to include them in the program. Tom said that he would talk it over with Louise, and Baxter had not insisted.

He opens the door to the darkroom and peers in. The muted crimson light from the single bulb illuminates the interior like a dull lantern in a cave. Baxter steps to the pans where the last prints are floating. He removes them, shakes some of the fluids from them and then clips them to a wire to dry. One of the photographs is of a dead horse covered with flies. The other is of a woman of thirty or so being restrained by two soldiers from rushing somewhere. She has the look of a woman who must get to where she wants to go or die trying. Baxter suddenly remembers the circumstance. A car bomb had detonated in front of her apartment house, and she was desperate to know if her children had survived. Both of the children had been killed, and the soldiers knew that. Hence their effort to restrain her. And at that second Baxter had taken the photograph.

It is in the darkroom while he is working on prints and negatives that he keeps asking himself why he went to Lebanon in the first place. What drew him to such a country? Was it just the old photographer's curse to be where the story was actually happening and not to feel fully alive unless he was actually there? Was it something else, something more? The answer eluded him.

And it is also at such times that he realizes but cannot admit to himself that he is by nature and disposition a born mate. Since the death of Mercedes he has tried to maintain the habits of his life, and, as long as his work occupied him, he has been successful. He has even proved to himself that he is self-sufficient. But at other times he has discovered the opposite. In those moments just before sleep or when he lacked the energy or even the desire to work in the darkroom or to aim his camera at anything, he has experienced the loneliness of the widower. Occasionally it has brought him to tears, or it has made him seethe with desolation and anger so that he has had to leave the house at all hours of the night and walk for miles in any direction in the hope that being in motion would exhaust his mood.

Once, while he was rummaging through a box of old photographs, he came across the photographs of a young woman whom he had photographed in the nude. He dawdled over the photographs. It made him think how much he missed looking at the female body. Mercedes had always been almost casual about being naked, and he had become used to seeing her that way after a shower or else lying supine on top of a sheeted bed to cool off on a humid day. He would relish the pleasure of looking at the soft swellings of her breasts and the graceful hump of her hip when she lay on her side. Scenes like that had been a part of his life with her, and they satisfied him as a man and also nourished his photographer's eye. The sight of her without clothes removed the veil of false modesty in their lives and eased something in his body that was related to a different desire than his desire to make love to her.

Occasionally he did take photographs of her in the nude, although she made him promise that they would be for him alone. It was not that she was ashamed at having posed for him. For her, nudity was related to intimacy, and she was not interested in being nude for any other reason. He assured her that he felt the same way, but she was still uneasy in front of the camera.

Having chanced upon the photographs of the nude model forced Baxter to realize how much the absence of Mercedes mattered to him physically. For months after her death he had thought of himself almost as a pure spirit. He remembered conversations they had had together, remem-

bered silences they shared when they were on trips together
or when they were drinking morning coffee, remembered
her moods, her ability to project herself into the anguish as
well as the joy of others. He rarely thought of her sexually.
But the photographs of the nude model reminded him of
Mercedes during those times when she posed for him or
when he watched her combing her hair while she stood
naked in front of a mirror or when she gave herself to him
on those cool nights as the wind through the opened windows lifted the curtains almost in rhythm with their kisses
and movements. Remembering Mercedes aroused Baxter
in ways he had temporarily forgotten or suppressed. The
desire lingered for days. And he knew that it would not go
away but only intensify.

For Baxter, fidelity in marriage meant not fidelity to the
idea of marriage or to some other abstraction but fidelity to
Mercedes herself. He retained that fidelity to her even after
her death. And yet the chance viewing of the photographs
of the nude model convinced him that he could not live like
a celibate for the rest of his life. The possibility of another
marriage not only never occurred to him, but it did not
interest him. He knew that his days with Mercedes were
unrepeatable, and his devotion to her excluded in advance
anything that might compete with that devotion in the future. His conclusion was that he would keep his memory of
Mercedes sacrosanct and deal with the waxings and wanings
of desire as he would deal with any other hunger of the
body. And he would see to it, he told himself, that these two
aspects of his behavior would remain separate.

In his life as a photographer, Baxter had occasion to meet
a variety of women. Since his reputation was international,

he usually found himself recognized wherever he went. With recognition went a certain notoriety, and with notoriety came opportunities for liaisons with women he could pursue if he so chose. When Mercedes was alive, he overlooked them. In fact, they had no appeal for him whatsoever. But more than a year after her death, his loneliness counterbalanced his previous feelings of indifference and aversion. After all, he thought, appetites were appetites. If he considered them simply for what they were, he would find a way to deal with them, but he would see to it that they would have no connection at all with his personal life. It took two separate occasions to convince him that this was impossible.

The first happened quite accidentally. He was en route to Nice via Paris to attend a symposium on silence. The topic intrigued him. Only the French, he told himself, could have conceived of a symposium on such a subject, and he wanted to attend to see if there would be included in the program any consideration of photography. Baxter always thought of it as a silent art because it grew out of a speechless interchange between photographer and subject.

He never reached Nice. Sitting opposite him in the first-class section of the Air France 747 was an actress whom he had met years earlier while attending a production of *King Lear* in Stratford, Connecticut. At that time she had implored him to photograph her so that she would have a "smashing picture" in her portfolio. She said she knew him by reputation, and she was convinced that a photograph of her by him would help her launch her career. More to be free of her than to accommodate her, he took a series of portraits in natural light, printed them when he returned to his home and mailed a set to her without charge. He never heard from her after that. But within five years she did become the nationally known actress she told him she would be. She'd changed her name in the process as well as her hair color from brown to blond and, if Baxter remembered correctly, her nose. She glanced at him several times across the aisle but gave no sign of recognizing him. When the plane landed in Paris, Baxter found himself standing beside her as they were about to disembark.

"Your pictures *did* help," she said straightforwardly.

He looked at her and smiled.

"I was wondering all the way across the Atlantic," she continued, "if you were going to speak to me or act as if we'd never met."

"What name should I use? The old one or the new one?"

"The new one. The world knows me that way. I know myself that way now." She handed a portfolio she was carrying to a younger woman, apparently her secretary, and told her to go ahead and claim the luggage. She then removed sunglasses from her purse, put them on, and covered her hair and the lower part of her face with a brown silk scarf. "I have to do this," she told Baxter as they walked.

After they had cleared the passport station together, Baxter was about to head for his connecting flight to Nice when she said, "Aren't you staying in Paris?"

"Not this time, Blanche." The falsity of her new name when he said it made him smile. He felt momentarily like an actor in a play. "I'm on my way to Nice."

She pretended she did not hear him. "I'm staying at the

Intercontinental. I'd like to see you later this evening if you're free. I'll have slept off this lag by then."

Baxter looked at her skeptically, but he saw at once that she was serious, and he saw as well what a woman who extends such an invitation to a man wants the man to see. He could have told her again that he was going to Nice just before she turned toward the limousine that was waiting for her, but he did not. An hour later he was registering at a hotel on the rue Jacob, and twelve hours after that he was knocking at the door of her suite at the Intercontinental.

While he waited, he noticed that the hallway smelled heavily of roses. When Blanche opened the door and stood there in a white bathrobe, he smelled the musk of roses to the exclusion of everything else. But once he was in the living room of the suite, he saw that there was not a rose in sight.

"Let me do something to my hair," she said, "and I'll be right back."

"Somebody must have sent you all the roses in France," he said, puzzled.

"Not roses. Rose water. I just took a bath in it. I love it."

"Judging from the aroma here, you must love it a lot."

He was standing at the window and contemplating the lights in the Hôtel Meurice across the street when he felt her arms around him. She put her cheek against his back and embraced him tightly. The smell of roses was everywhere.

"I don't play games, Bax," she said. "You helped me a lot, so I'd like to pay you back. My way. Then we'll be quits."

"I didn't realize there even was a debt."

"Sshh," she whispered. "No arguments. Nobody's forcing you. I want it this way."

The fact that what was happening was happening so quickly gave Baxter the excuse he needed not to think about it. He felt himself acquiescing even as she spoke, and when she led him to the bedroom, he knew that he was as ripe for what was about to happen as she was. At least he told himself that. It was only after he kissed her that his head started to clear. He began to think. To stop his mind before it went any further, he kissed her harder, shaped his hand to her bath-cooled breast and then touched her softly below the navel and down and between and back. The light from the bathroom slashed across them. He saw that her eyes were closed and that she was writhing softly with the pleasure that he was giving her. Gradually his desire for her ebbed. He wanted to want her but somehow could not. He tried to adopt her mood. Nothing. He still forced himself to continue. Her face moved in and out of the light, and she continued to keep her eyes closed, but loosely, as if she were asleep and in the grip of a delicious dream. Baxter realized at that moment that anybody could be playing with her, that he was just serving her needs at the moment. She reached down and guided him into her. She looked at him, her eyes almost sad with the pleasure that was mounting in her.

Baxter returned her look, but he saw that she was not really looking at him. Her eyes were simply open, and that was all. Almost in revenge he thrust himself into her with some force, but it was an act without passion. He felt less himself than he had ever felt before in his life, and in his anger he loosed himself into her without any sense of relief or accomplishment. At the same time, he felt her shivering in a series of spasms beneath him and gripping his arms and jerking her head from side to side on the bed and even whimpering in bursts.

The telephone on the table beside the bed rang. While they were still joined, she reached for the phone and put it to her ear. She closed her eyes and listened but did not say hello. Finally she said, "I'm listening, Pierre. Just come to the point."

Slowly the expression on her face changed. She was weighing carefully whatever Pierre was telling her and nodding yes or nodding no to herself. Baxter eased himself out of her and sat on the edge of the bed. She started talking to Pierre as if Baxter were no longer in the room. The bedclothes slid to the floor. Baxter turned slightly and faced her. Her eyes were still closed, and she was talking rapidly in dollars and cents. Baxter looked at her body from the breastbone to the ankles. He thought of what he would be doing at that moment in Nice. Then he stood, slipped on his underwear, his suit, socks and shoes and walked to the door and opened it.

"Good-bye, Blanche," he said.

Without interrupting her conversation, Blanche lifted her free hand and, with her eyes still closed, clenched and unclenched her fingers in an Italian good-bye in the direction of Baxter's voice. Baxter closed the door and left like someone turning over the last page of a book he never should have started to read in the first place. He still smelled of rose water, which clung to him like a brand. It would be four days before he could wash away the scent completely.

The second incident happened with a photographer named Mitzi. She and Baxter had known one another for years as co-professionals, and Baxter admired her work, particularly her photographs of children. Although Mitzi spoke frequently of wanting to marry and "of leaving photography for the weekends," she had a propensity for falling frequently but unhappily and sometimes disastrously in love. One of her lovers beat her with her camera case before leaving her. Another left her pregnant. She dutifully bore the child and convinced her mother to help her raise it. It was not that Mitzi was a fool. Baxter had always found her as intelligent as she was competent. She was simply unlucky in her relationships with men, and her need for affection blinded her to the failings in certain men who victimized or abused her.

Baxter met up with her three years after Mercedes' death when he flew to Mexico City to photograph the results of a quake there. He had photographed many instances of quake damage along the fault that ran from the Aleutians down through California and then snaked into Mexico and South America. It was not the destruction as such that interested Baxter as a photographer but the expressions on the faces of the survivors. He looked particularly for that resoluteness that kept despair at bay. Occasionally he found it.

He had been in a damaged suburb north of Mexico City for less than a day when he saw Mitzi. She told him she had actually been there during the earthquake, and she even showed him some of the photographs she took while it was happening. She told him that she'd heard about his wife. Later that evening they had dinner together in the dining room of his hotel. During dinner there were tremors. Baxter and Mitzi and the other diners evacuated the hotel and ran for the hills. When the second series of tremors came, they watched from the hills as the hotel listed like a bombed ship and its rear wall caved in.

When the tremors ceased, Mitzi told Baxter that her hotel was in a part of town that had not been affected and suggested that he try to find a room there. She did not reckon with the fact that others would have the same idea. With the hotel totally booked, Mitzi suggested that Baxter stay on the balcony in her room. There was a lounge there, and it was as good as a bed.

After midnight the tremors began again. Baxter had just fallen asleep, and he woke to find Mitzi standing beside the lounge and shivering.

"My God, Bax, we're going to die down here. We really are."

Baxter felt the building shudder with each new tremor. He sat up on the lounge as Mitzi cowered beside him, holding his arm the way a child might hold a parent's hand during a thunderstorm.

"I'm not very brave, Bax. I saw what the first quake did last Saturday in the city. These buildings down here are just made out of sand and spit."

"It's not as bad as all that."

"It's worse, believe me. I know."

The tremors eased. Baxter stood and went to the balcony railing. He saw that all the buildings across the street were intact. A few people were running back and forth between the buildings.

"There's not a light anywhere," said Baxter.

"Maybe the cables were cut," said Mitzi. "That happens all the time. A quake does a lot of damage underground too."

She came and stood beside him at the railing. Together they peered into the darkness.

"I'm such a baby about these things, Bax," she said. "Riots I deal with. War I can deal with, but not earthquakes."

She was standing close enough to Baxter for him to feel her shivering like someone unable to get warm. He put his arm around her, but the shivering did not cease. She stood even closer to him, and he held her as if he were comforting someone bereaved.

After a few moments he felt her turn to him in the darkness. The shivering was almost gone. "Bax," she said, and her voice was her normal voice again. "You know, Bax, I always had a hell of a crush on you. I just never let it show." She put her arms around his waist and placed her cheek against his chest. He responded almost automatically. He could feel that she was wearing nothing under her knee-length nightgown. Mitzi began to kiss his chest, the tip of his chin.

"Come on, Mitzi," said Baxter, "we have too much on one another to go ahead like this. Especially now."

"Says who?" answered Mitzi between kisses.

Slowly she raised her face to his and kissed him on the mouth, her lips softening against his and separating as the kiss went on. He could taste her breath. Suddenly she was an answer. After the travel, the tremors and the months of work and solitude, he felt himself wanting her, even needing her.

Together they lay down on the lounge. He inhaled the scent of her in the darkness, the tart odor of her hair, the punctual warmth of her breathing. In a matter of moments they made a small, tight knot of their bodies under the moon-centered Mexican sky.

Later, as they lay side by side on the lounge, Baxter asked, "Are you cold?"

"A little, but who cares . . ."

"We're too old for this, Mitzi."

"Speak for yourself. It was great for me."

"I don't mean this. I mean after this."

"Just take it as it comes, Bax. I'll be there when you need me."

"You didn't tell that to the other guys in your life, did you?"

"They were bastards."

"How do you know I'm not one?"

"Not a chance, Bax."

"You've been wrong before, Mitzi."

"You're doing your best to spoil the mood, do you know that?"

"I'm sorry."

"Don't be sorry. Just be satisfied."

They slept without exchanging another word. When they woke in the morning, they both felt a certain awkwardness. Mitzi repeated some of the assurances she had said to him during the night. Baxter did not answer. As they both packed their bags, they realized without saying so that they had nothing more to exchange with one another or to give one another. Whatever had drawn them together during the night kept receding and receding. By the time they reached the airport, it was as if nothing had ever happened between them.

They took separate flights from Mexico City back to the States, she to Los Angeles, he to New York. He never saw her again.

O YOU WANT ME TO FACE THIS CAMERA or the one over there?" asks Baxter. He is seated on a hip-high stool between two mounted photographs that Louise has selected to use for the concluding segment of the program.

"The camera directly in front of you," says Louise. "When the red light comes on just to the left of the lens, it means the tape is running. Talk directly to the lens. The other camera will be shooting you at the same time, and we'll cut and mix later. Don't worry about the second camera. I'll take care of that. Just speak to the first one as if you're talking to someone you've known for a long time. Imagine that you're talking to Tom."

"When do you want me to start?"

"When the red light comes on, Mr. Baxter. They're making a last check. Could you say something so that they can get a level, please?"

"I'm not good at this. I hope you realize that I'm better on the other side of a camera and not on this side of it."

"That's perfect."

"What's perfect?"

"I mean the voice level is perfect. Now the best way to approach this segment is just to talk about photography in general, then about specific pictures like the ones we have mounted here, then about being a photographer. Be relaxed. Just be as natural as possible. Try to forget that you're on camera. The rest will take care of itself."

"You're more optimistic than I am," answers Baxter, shifting his weight on the stool.

"The light is on, Mr. Baxter. You can begin any time now."

Baxter looks directly at the red Cyclops eye on the camera in front of him. He finds that he cannot speak to it. He shakes his head.

"Try to imagine that you're speaking to a friend, Mr. Baxter," says Louise.

"It's hard to imagine. All I see is a piece of equipment. That's not something I respond to. Maybe we should think of a different way to end the program."

"Would it help if I stood just to the left of the cameraman? You can talk directly to me."

Baxter looks at the red light and then at Louise. He ignores the camera entirely and directs his remarks to Louise. "These photographs," he begins, indicating the mounted photographs on his left and right, "these photographs were taken in Lebanon. Some of you might consider them good examples of photojournalism, but for me they are failures."

Louise looks at him with surprise. She has never heard him say these words before, and she wonders if his reluctance to film this part of the program has provoked him to such a point that he might ruin it for her.

"I don't mean the pictures are failures photographically," Baxter is saying. "As photographs they aren't bad, I suppose. The composition. The arrangement. The cropping. These elements are not bad. But neither of them convey what I hoped to convey. Neither of them is the picture I wanted to take in Lebanon. The only way I can explain that untaken picture is to say a few things about Lebanon itself. As you know, as most of you know, Lebanon is a country that's being torn apart. It reminds me of a prisoner whose arms and legs are tied to four horses, and the horses are pulling the prisoner's limbs in four different directions. I don't have to elaborate on that image, I'm sure.

"But for me, Lebanon is in miniature what any country might become, even our country. We can't imagine that happening here because we still have a healthy respect for the law, and we still trust our institutions. But suppose that something happens that takes away our respect for the law and our trust in our institutions. What's there to fill in the vacuum? Force. Force and counterforce. Since that's what governs relations between most of the countries of this world, that shouldn't come as too much of a surprise to us. But just suppose that force and counterforce become the dominant powers *within* a country. In that kind of a country the only law becomes the law of the gun. The Old West was that kind of a society for quite a long time. The man with the gun was king, and everyone who didn't have a gun lived in fear of the man who did.

"I for one have always been sympathetic to those people who have to live under the gun, who have to live in fear. If they can't find guns of their own to equalize the situation, then they just go on living at the will of the gunman. It's as simple as that. Well, the various factions in Lebanon compensated for that a while ago. Every faction has its own arms. Every faction has a turf. And there is a kind of primitive form of checks and balances that operates among the factions. It's not so much a question of one faction conquering the other as it is a matter of no faction getting the upperhand. What results is a kind of balance. It's a bloody balance, but it's a balance nonetheless." Baxter pauses, looks down at his hands and then resumes. "My own view is that the situation in Lebanon is what can happen when law and national trust erode and when arms are available. People end up living in a chaos of turmoil and horror. It could happen in Italy. It could happen in France. It could happen right here. It might take a little longer for it to happen here because of our size and because our institutions have more durability, but it remains a possibility.

"This possibility has led me to believe that Lebanonization will be a major threat in the world for the rest of the century and even beyond. I mean Lebanonization on an international scale. It's the one possibility that's the most feasible, and it's within the capacity of anyone within any country who has the will to make it happen. The other possibilities are the ones we hear about most and the ones we defend ourselves against. I mean nuclear war and what is called conventional war. But Lebanonization is a war that comes from within, and it's like a weed. It can grow anywhere at all.

"We've all read of instances where some disturbed man holes up in a tower or walks into a public building or a restaurant and starts shooting up the place. We know what that does to the community. People start to look over their shoulders. They look at strangers suspiciously. But let's multiply that incident by a number of incidents. And let's assume that the people behind these incidents have a plan for random destruction and that they have allies and that many of these allies of theirs are even willing to give up their lives to create that kind of random destruction at places of their choosing anywhere in the country. Can you imagine the effect this would have on all of us? And then suppose that these acts were repeated over a period of weeks or months. The whole of our society would begin to strain at the seams. Our sense of social confidence would begin to weaken. And since a democracy is built on trust and confidence, the whole of our way of life would be under duress. For me that's a horrible prospect. And unless you've been in Lebanon you have no idea how horrible that prospect can be. It's militia versus militia, sect versus sect, neighborhood versus neighborhood, house versus house. Just when you think that the savagery and cruelty can go no further, you discover that they can go further. Just when you think the tempo of chaos will change for the better, it changes for the worse. You start to live from day to day. Then from hour to hour. Then, at the worst times, from breath to breath." Baxter pauses again and clears his throat. He shifts his weight on the stool and once again looks at the camera, then at Louise. He cannot tell what she thinks of what he is saying, but he notes that she is frowning. Regardless, he is so caught up in his own logic that he goes right on. "I wanted to take one photograph in Lebanon that showed the look in people's faces when they thought they were taking their last breath. For me that single photograph would have shown to the whole world the face that all of us have hidden behind our everyday faces. These photographs that are mounted on either side of me don't show that. They show the look on people's faces after the worst has happened to them, not while it is happening or at that split second when it is about to happen. The photograph I didn't take would have showed people on the verge. And if my theory about Lebanonization is right, then we're all on the verge, but we don't realize it. The photograph that I wanted to take—"

"Cut," interrupts Louise.

Baxter looks at her as she steps in front of the camera. "Something wrong?" he asks. "Was I looking at the right spot?"

"No, Mr. Baxter, that part of it was fine. But what you're saying is not in keeping with the rest of the program. It's much too political."

"Political?"

"I mean it's much too concerned with the *situation* over there. You're really not talking about photography at all. You're talking more about history, about—"

"Maybe you weren't listening closely enough to what I was saying, Louise. I didn't say a word that can be separated from my theory of photography. It just so happens that history and photography coincide in this instance. And besides that, there are deeper implications. I regard the situation in Lebanon as a symptom of something that could be international. The tragedy of Lebanon is exportable."

"That may very well be true, Mr. Baxter. But the program is not really concerned with that."

Baxter slides off the stool and walks closer to Louise. He seems less annoyed than perplexed by her position. "What do you want me to do then? What do you want me to say?"

"Well, something that would be in keeping with the theme of the rest of the program. Maybe you could talk about the place of photography in your life or the importance that you think it has in society."

"But I did."

"It might have seemed that way to you, Mr. Baxter, but it didn't come through that way. It came across like a talk in international relations, not photography."

"Well, Louise, I think we have a basic difference of view here," says Baxter. "You asked me in the beginning to be perfectly natural, and that's what I was. I can't do it any other way. I can't talk about something I don't feel."

"I understand that, but could you just approach what you're talking about from another perspective?"

"No, I couldn't. There is no other perspective. Not for me."

"Well, in that case, Mr. Baxter, I guess we have no choice except to use what we have. It's not what I would have preferred, but it will have to do."

"I guess it will."

Baxter shrugs and walks past the camera to the exit. He can feel Louise's eyes as well as the eyes of the entire crew on him. He opens the exit door, pauses and turns. Everyone is watching him, and Louise is standing exactly where he left her.

"Good night, Louise," he says quietly.

"Good night, Mr. Baxter."

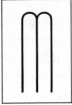

AYBE I WAS TOO HARD ON HER. But the real
fact is that I've gotten closer to her than I've
wanted. It's not true that you learn about a
woman only when you live with her. You can
learn a lot about a woman if you work with
her. And working with her for the past three
months has made me feel more like myself than I've felt in
years. Sometimes I've just wanted to talk to her alone, but
I talked myself out of it. But I always looked forward to
seeing her at the studio the next day. I'm making too much

out of what I said to her back there. It was just a little disagreement. Why is it eating at me? We've disagreed before, and we've worked things out on the job. This isn't any different. I said what I had to say, and there's nothing more to say. If she doesn't understand it, that's too bad. That's the way I see things. She can just cut and edit it any old way she wants, but I'm not going to go back and do it again. Still, I knew that I'd hurt her by saying what I said in front of the crew. I could see it in her face. She really deserved better than that. She's done a hell of a job so far. All right, maybe I wasn't fair to her. But the truth is that I'm afraid to give her an inch. It would just take that much for things to get personal between us. She knows too much about me. But I don't want her to know that I was the one who made is possible for Mercedes to be killed. She'd try to sympathize, and then I'd try to explain that I was just taking pictures and that the pictures were good and that I got so caught up in what I was doing that I didn't even think of the danger. I was like the gambler playing for the last, big winning hand, but it was one hand too many. And Mercedes had to pay for it. She just happened to be in the way of a single bullet, and I saw her go down, and I couldn't, for God's sake, believe it. She'd just been talking to me. I'd just heard her voice. I've dreamed that scene so many times that there's not a surprise in it anymore, but there is the same pain in it, and every time it gets worse. There are times when I feel I just have to talk to somebody about it and say that what happened was the last thing that I wanted to happen. I even pray to Mercedes to forgive me. I pray to God to forgive me because her death is with me all the time even though I know that what happened happened just because it happened. Things like that happen. There's no blame involved in it. I keep telling myself that. But I still blame myself because I didn't leave when I should have. I just had to take that last damned picture, and that picture killed her. But I've never told that to a soul, not even to Tom. I try not even to tell myself except at times like right now when I'm strong enough to take it. Even though she's buried, I still stay married to Mercedes. I'll be that way for the rest of my life. Those women in Paris and Mexico—I just let my loneliness get the better of me. I tell myself it was just the male in me, but that's not the truth. I knew what I was doing. I could have walked away before things happened if I wanted to. I just didn't want to. And in this work there are always women in the wings, attractive women, intelligent women, and they all have that vertical mouth just where their thighs meet, and a man fits there as if it's the answer to everything. But it doesn't wash off the next day. At least for me it doesn't wash off. I try to put that part of myself on indefinite hold, and I go on with my work because when I'm working I always feel like a novice no matter how good the last photographs were. I'm always learning something I didn't know. And I feel saved from the past because my work tells me that the best photographs are still waiting to be taken. And just like that I'm thinking of the future again. And I tell myself I have to stay alert because the opportunity for the best photograph can happen just like that. I keep the camera around my neck, and I keep looking and waiting. I'm in harness. My work turns into my permanent address. It's almost like a pilgrimage. All I travel with are my cameras and a satchelful of clothes, and that's when I feel I'm alive again. That's why I went to

Lebanon. That's something that Louise can't understand. You have to have lived through it to understand it, and even then you don't understand it. But you know that it could happen anywhere because human beings are really no different anywhere. Who would have ever thought that hell could happen in Lebanon? They called it the Switzerland of the Middle East. And it was. But it turned into hell by the sea. And it's still that way. I saw it. I was there. I saw it with Biggie, and Biggie's still there. Poor Biggie. When the napalm got him, I felt I was losing my brother all over again. And then I had to see him dead and burned black, and the face that used to be Biggie's face was like tissue paper and cindery as the face of some Egyptian mummy. And everybody else was burned into ebony, and the smell was beyond description. I just pointed the camera and clicked the shutter while everybody else was screaming or running around to see who was left alive. But once I saw that the napalm got Biggie, I didn't care who was still alive. It was all subject matter to me then. It was just human geography. And all the time I was working, I kept remembering what Biggie told me about Afghanistan. He said that the Russians used napalm there, and the Afghans had no defense against it. But once, he said, the Afghans got even by dynamiting both ends of a tunnel while a Russian battalion was passing through it in a troop train. The dynamite sealed both ends airtight, and the Afghans just left the Russians corked in there. When Biggie got to the spot two weeks later, he got the Afghans to open up one end of the tunnel, and he went in with some irregulars and a stringer from *Stern.* He said that there seemed to be the whole battalion piled up like cordwood, body on top of body on

top of body, just at the entrance as if each soldier wanted
to be the first to get out if an opening suddenly happened.
It smelled like a charnel house in there, so Biggie just
worked the flash for about fifteen minutes so he'd have the
evidence, and the irregulars went around confiscating
weapons and ammunition and boots and belts and whatever
else they might be able to use. Then they sealed up the
opening like a tomb and went back to the war. Now Biggie's gone, and I don't even know where he's buried. I
learned later that he was bulldozed into a trough with all
the rest of the dead, and that was that. No marker. Nothing.
Of course, he gave every day a run for its money. Good
food. The best Scotch he could find. And any woman who
was willing. In Beirut he kept telling me again and again
that no two women came in the same way. He said there
was one in London who burst into tears when it happened
to her and kept crying for more than an hour. And there
was one in Tokyo whose leg reflexes were so strong that he
couldn't lean over to tie his shoes for a week. That was
Biggie. He worked hard, and he played hard. He used to
say he didn't care about AIDS or anything else. In his kind
of work he felt he earned a good lay once in a while, and
so he'd reward himself his way. It didn't matter who the
woman was. When Mercedes was alive, I always felt a little
sorry for Biggie. It was so easy to see what was missing in
his life, and why he kept on the prowl as he did. I told him
once without any trimmings that he was just wasting the
best part of his life, and he told me to shut up. Then he said
I was one of the lucky ones because I had someone. That's
all he ever said. After Mercedes died, I realized that I was
really worse off than Biggie because I'd lost the only some-

one I loved while Biggie never had anyone to lose. I could compare then and now, but Biggie had nothing there to compare. For months after I buried Mercedes I thought I'd go crazy. I couldn't face my own mind. I couldn't outthink myself. Then after a year or so I started to think that what Mercedes and I had together might happen in a different way for me with another woman. I even thought I could find someone like her. But, of course, that didn't happen. Those things never happen. Nobody can wish somebody made to order to put your life back together again. Then I had my first understanding of what tragedy meant . . . tragedy for me. The only one who's taken my mind off myself for the past three months is Louise. She's nothing like Mercedes so it's not a question of similarities. It's just that she always talks to me as if only right now matters. There's no alternative. And I want to know more about her and be with her more, but something always makes me hold back. I almost think I'm afraid. She's not the same as Blanche, and she's certainly no Mitzi, and the one thing I don't want to do with her is follow that old, dry dream of stifling my loneliness in another woman's body because it just doesn't stifle anything. It only makes things worse and a lot more sordid. But you don't find that out until afterward. In the beginning you just tell yourself that it's only biology. It's better to be satisfied than always to be a hostage to your own feelings. You even tell yourself that morality and sex are two separate questions. You tell yourself all kinds of things, and they're all lies. Blanche was a lie, and Mitzi was a lie. I don't know if Louise is a lie or not, but I don't know how to proceed. Maybe the answer will come to me. Maybe I should go away for a month or so and let a little time and distance clarify my thinking. I'll get in touch with her when I come back. Tom said a lot of good things about her. I think he was trying to tell me that she had some feelings for me. He's known her longer . . . I can't read history or philosophy anymore, and I can't listen to ministers or priests or to religious people. They're just not in touch with the world I know. It all sounds like escapism to me. Everything does except photography. When you're a photographer, you know that the world you see through a lens is all the world that matters, and it's in motion all the time so you have to focus on it all the time. And then you realize that you're a part of it, and if you let your lens be your nose and let it lead you, you might be lucky enough to come up with an answer once in a while. It starts to influence your whole life. You don't think just with your head but with your eyes and your fingers and your nose and your mouth and your ears. That's the only theology that makes any sense. That's what real intelligence means. I can still hear my father telling me that Diogenes believed that knowledge was not intelligence and that it could never be intelligence until it became as real as your next breath. And then he told me that he named me after Diogenes just so I'd be reminded all my life of that fact. I guess it all comes down to wisdom. Maybe I'm just not wise enough. That could be the problem. I keep telling myself that it's just not wise to let someone into my heart again. And if Louise is that someone, then I can't let her in. It would mean taking the risk of losing her. That sounds like it's close to the truth. I just don't want to risk losing someone I love again. It would be a thousand times worse. But then how can you live if you never take a risk?"

14

OM, BAXTER AND LOUISE have just finished watching the final version of *Stills in Motion.* As the credits slide up the screen, they look at one another. Tom and Louise seem to be awaiting a reaction from Baxter. Baxter simply looks at them both and smiles.

"Well," says Tom finally, "have we done you justice?"

"You know I'm no judge, Tom."

"Come on, Bax, you can't hide behind that dodge any more. How did you like it?"

"For someone who's come back from the dead, I don't think I have any right to complain."

"Please, Mr. Baxter," interjects Louise. "We really need you to be frank with us. The next ones to see this program will be the public. If there is anything that you think needs to be changed, now is the time to change it."

"No changes, Louise," says Baxter and stands. "It's not a matter of change for me at all. It's just that I have a real allergy against this type of publicity."

"It's not publicity, Mr. Baxter. We scrupulously tried to avoid anything that smacks of that."

"But the fact is that it's making me public. I'm the one being revealed to total strangers in this program, and I can't quite feel comfortable about that."

"Have we shown something that you object to?" asks Louise.

"No, it's not one single thing. It's the whole concept. The program puts me front and center and not my work, and I think it's my work that's important."

Tom looks at Louise and shrugs. His shoulders say, *What's the use of talking since it's really too late now.*

"Well, Bax," says Tom. "I'm off. My family's waiting for me. I hope you think differently about this tomorrow. I think you will." He turns to Louise. "I think you've done a superb job, Louise. I couldn't have asked for more. I'll see you tomorrow morning, and we'll talk about distribution."

After Tom leaves the studio, Louise busies herself with rewinding the film. She senses that Baxter is watching her, but she pretends to be oblivious. When she finally finishes rewinding, she turns to see Baxter still looking at her.

"Well," she sighs, "that's that."

"Are you sad when a job's over?" he asks.

"It's hard not to be."

"What will you do now?"

"Get involved with another project, I suppose. Tom will come up with something."

Louise picks up her purse and starts in the direction of the studio exit.

"Are you going home?" asks Baxter.

"I think I'll walk. I need the exercise."

"May I walk with you?"

Louise pauses momentarily. She is having a difficult time reconciling the Baxter in front of her with the Baxter who was so dismissive about the program only moments before.

"If you like," says Louise.

"I would."

After leaving the building they walk in silence for almost a block. Several times Louise brings herself to the verge of saying something, but each time she backs down. She would like nothing better than to tell Baxter what it is about him that bothers her. Then she would like to ask him why he persists in keeping such a professional distance between them that only he is able to define and then suddenly redefine simply by asking her if he can walk her to her apartment. She even would like to tell him that she thinks his plunging himself into his work in one dangerous situation after another strikes her as a pursuit of death, not life, and that he is kidding himself if he thinks otherwise.

"Tom told me you're married," says Baxter.

"*Was* married," answers Louise, startled. She never expected their conversation to start like this. She wonders what Baxter will ask her next.

"That's right," he says, remembering. "I think Tom told me that."

"We just weren't suited. We weren't a pair. It was simple as that. I realized it before Harry did. My husband's name . . . my ex-husband's name is Harry. In fact, Harry didn't realize it at all. But he's found someone else now, so that's that."

Louise surprises herself by being so quick to divulge these facts. She tells herself that she will be more restrained.

"I hope you don't mind my question," says Baxter softly. "For the past few months we've only talked shop. I thought it might be better for both of us if we turned to another channel. If you want to, I mean . . ."

"No problem, Mr. Baxter."

Louise feels that Baxter is either probing for something or else he just wants to talk. In either case she feels uneasy. What could be on his mind? Why has he waited until now to show her this side of himself?

"I think I've been Mr. Baxter long enough," says Baxter. "Everyone else calls me Bax. I'd appreciate it if you would call me Bax. After all, I call you Louise."

Louise takes two more steps and stops. She doesn't know if she is being patronized or not, but she feels her anger rising. "Mr. Baxter, I'm not the one—"

"Bax . . ."

"Bax, I'm not the one who set up the rules between us. If you remember correctly, you did that from the beginning. And you kept it that way while we worked together. And now that the job is over, you want to change the rules. Well, to be frank with you, I don't think that's quite fair of you. Just half an hour ago you didn't have a good word to say about a film that's taken the better part of half a year to finish. And I was involved in that effort every step of the way. I can't help but take that personally. I worked harder on that than I've worked on anything in my entire life . . ."

"I didn't mean for you to take my remarks personally. I was talking about the program itself. I'm really not concerned with that kind of thing. It doesn't mean that much to me."

"Well, it means a lot to me. It means a lot to Tom as well. It was his idea. And that should make it mean something to you even if nothing else does." She feels her voice getting higher and louder. Noticing that an oncoming jogger with maroon weights in either hand is striding toward them, she pauses. When the jogger passes out of earshot, Louise continues, "I think I'll go the rest of the way by myself." She is speaking normally now. "But in all honesty, Mr. Baxter, you say the most unsettling things sometimes. And I don't even think that you realize the effect they have on a person."

She wheels and hurries down the block toward her apartment. She is almost running, and she feels that she will either cry or swear, so perplexed and overwrought is she by her own frustration and fury. By the time she reaches her apartment, she is perspiring. She closes the door behind her, leans against it and flings her purse on the floor near the sofa.

"Damn him," she says aloud. After a few moments she goes to sit on the edge of the sofa where she begins to cry in spasms as if she has just received momentous bad news. She is still crying when there is a light knock on the door.

"Yes," she says, composing herself.

"It's Bax."

"Please, go away."

"Well, I'm not."

"Go away, please. I don't want to see you right now. Honestly I don't."

"But I'd like to see you, Louise. It seems that I've stepped on your feelings without realizing it, and I wouldn't want things to end this way."

Louise wipes the tears from her eyes with the back of her right hand, walks slowly and erectly to the door and opens it. Then, leaving the door open behind her, she returns to the sofa and sits down tensely.

Baxter enters and seats himself in a chair opposite her. He looks at her directly for some time, but she averts her eyes.

"It's not that I'm against what you did on the film, Louise," he says. He is choosing his words carefully. "As a film, I think it's quite acceptable, quite good. It's just that I find the whole business embarrassing . . ."

"But why do you feel that way? It's not an embarrassment, Bax. It's not, not at all." She speaks his name with a firmness that surprises him and her as well. "It's just that you keep wanting to bury yourself, keep trying to put yourself in the past, keep acting like someone who is sick and tired of life around you, and this film keeps dragging you back into life. That's what you don't like about it. That's the problem." Louise stops to see how he will answer her, but Baxter says nothing. She places her palms on her knees and leans forward. All of her assessments of him during the past few months are arranging themselves for expression in her mind, and she knows that she must say them now, or she never will say them at all. "Bax, I don't think I've gotten to know any man as well as I've gotten to know you in the past year. I knew you even before I met you, and the man I came to know from the letters and the tape recordings and the photographs was a man I liked and admired. I liked and respected you, Bax. And in the beginning when we started to work together, we seemed to get along all right. It was formal, but we got along. After that I don't know what happened. I began to feel as if I were just a part of the set. You spoke to me only when you had to. You made sure there was always a third person present, and then you spoke to that person. What did I do? Did I say something or do something that made you treat me that way?"

"It was nothing you said or did, Louise. It was nothing like that at all," says Baxter. Her intensity has put him on the defensive, and he looks away.

"And on top of that, no matter what I suggested to improve the program, you made me feel as if I were intruding when I was just trying to do my job. I didn't ask to read your letters or your journal or listen to the tape you left for Tom. I even told Tom that I felt uncomfortable listening to a lot of those personal things. But he told me it was part of my job. And so I read and I listened. And after all those months, Bax, I did learn one thing about you, and it's going to kill me if I don't tell you." She pauses and draws a breath and holds it as if she is about to jump into darkness. Then she releases it and says, "You may have thought that you were out to photograph life as it was happening, but everything you did by going back to Lebanon wasn't going back to something but running away from something. I almost felt that you were hoping to die there. And that's suicidal, Bax. It was as if you wanted to snuff yourself out, erase yourself. When that occurred to me, I couldn't accept it. I had a picture of you as a man on the side of life. From your photographs I saw or thought I saw that you regarded people as human beings, not as nameless things in front of your camera. All your photographs said that to me. But the more I became aware of that suicidal streak in you, Bax, the more I started to think that you were just hiding behind your camera. You photographed people when you should have been helping them. You took pictures of them when they were suffering, and you even went looking for the suffering. What kind of a vision of life is that?"

"You don't understand, Louise. It's not what you think at all."

"Well, if I'm wrong, I'd really appreciate it if you straightened me out. I admire you a lot, Bax, and I don't want to feel the way I do. I even hate myself for talking like this to you, but I'm not made of wood. You can't be formal with me one minute and then switch to some other mood the next minute. You must know how I feel about you. You certainly must be able to sense that. I don't conceal it very well." She doesn't know if she will regret confessing this to him or not, but she cannot think of any reason to hide it. "Don't play with my feelings like that, Bax. It hurts. It hurts a lot."

Louise pauses and reaches for her purse and removes a handkerchief from it. She wipes her eyes with the handkerchief and then keeps the handkerchief wadded in her right hand. For several minutes she and Baxter sit facing one another in silence before Baxter rises from his chair and begins to pace the room slowly.

"Did Tom ever tell you how my wife died, Louise?"

Louise transfers the handkerchief from her right hand to her left. "He told me she died in Lebanon. A gunshot. That's all he ever said to me about her."

"She died because I was too damn busy taking pictures to realize that I was placing her in danger. She was killed because of me." He stops and faces her. "Because of me, Louise."

"I can't believe that, Bax."

"Not directly, maybe. But indirectly. And the guilt gets worse every week. It's tough enough to be without her, but I have to live with that memory."

"Bax, I know how you felt about your wife," says Louise, trying to counteract the momentum of his thought before it takes control of him. "I know how you felt about Mercedes. And what I didn't know Tom told me. So I don't think you should torture yourself like that."

"It's a hard thing to live with, Louise. And I don't know if I can ever get rid of it."

"Do you think you're living the way Mercedes would want you to live?" Louise is surprised at the way she keeps referring to Mercedes by name, as if she has been doing it for years. She notices that the sound of her name in the room silences Baxter momentarily.

"That's an impossible question to answer, Louise," he says, returning to his chair and sitting down.

"People die, Bax. The living can't die with them. The script isn't written that way. That sounds like a cliché, but there's no other way to put it."

"Loss is a terrible thing. A terrible thing. You don't know what it can do to you until it's done it. You can't prepare yourself. You can't rehearse. It wears you down." Baxter settles back in the chair like a man too exhausted by work or thought to care about anything except his own exhaustion. "When you're married to someone you love and then you lose them, you're still married to them. You stay married. Isn't that a remarkable thing about people? But the price you pay when they're gone is the longest loneliness in the world."

"And so you decided it was better to die in Lebanon or at least to risk dying. That way the problem would be solved for you once and for all." Louise is startled not only by her own frankness but also by her own insight. All that she has thought about Baxter for the past year is growing into definition in the very circumstance of their conversation. She feels that all her research has been a preparation for this moment.

"Is it as simple as that?"

"To me it is." Louise returns the handkerchief to her purse. "You're lucky you had the years with Mercedes that you had, Bax. At least you know that you had a real love once in your life. And if you still have that love for her even though she's gone, that only proves how real it was." She smooths the material in the sofa seat beside her. "My marriage was just the opposite of that."

"How?"

"Well, it's hard to put into words. Let's just say that when you're married to someone you don't love, then you were never really married in the first place. I can't think of any other way to say it."

"What's the answer?"

"I don't know, Bax." Louise lifts her shoulders and lets them fall limply. "I don't even know why we're talking like this. For months, just shoptalk. Then all of a sudden, we're talking from the heart. It's crazy."

"Maybe that's the answer."

"What?"

"Hearing yourself say what you're thinking, and then facing what you've just said."

"I don't know if it's as complicated as that, Bax. All I know is that you can't live with a load of regret on your back. You can't. And I can't. And what's more, I won't. It's like living in fear."

"It's not a question of fear to me," says Baxter. "It's almost too deep to talk about. I try to find words to say what I mean, and the words don't exist."

"I don't think it's as deep as you think it is. It really could be right in front of you. It could be that you're complicating what you can't accept."

Baxter stands and walks toward Louise. She expects him to sit down beside her on the sofa, but he keeps standing.

"Louise," he says, "for almost four years I've felt that a part of me has gone on ahead, has left me. I'm sure you can understand that. It happens to everybody at one time or another. I've come to the conclusion that I can't do anything about that. All I *can* do is deal with myself as I am now, deal with the part of me that's still left. And there have been times when it's torn me apart. Especially at night or when I'm tired and my defenses are down completely. A couple of times my body's caught up with me, and I've silenced it in some woman. Each time it was a different woman, but that's not important. It was with each of them just a concession. And it turned into a different kind of dying. I always felt worse afterward." He returns to his chair, starts to sit down, decides against it and walks in a small circle around the chair before he says, "Ever since I met you, Louise, I've fought against thinking of you as a . . . as a . . ."

"Concession?"

"Yes. I've fought against that. Maybe that's why I kept such a wall between us. I don't know. I couldn't think of anything safer to do. I didn't want to fall into old habits." He makes another circle around the chair. "You have a lot going for you, Louise, a lot more than you realize. And you've been a real help to me even though I haven't been able to say how. If I had the courage or whatever it was that I needed, I would have said this to you a long time ago. But with you I always questioned my motives. You're personal to me. You mean a lot to me. Not the way Mercedes was . . . is personal to me, but it's just as real as that. And it's just as important." He stops as if his well of words has gone dry. "I think the best thing for me to do is just to go away for a month or so until I sort out what's inside of me. But I wanted to tell you face-to-face how I felt before I left. It's presumptuous as hell, I know, and tomorrow you'll probably tell yourself that you've been listening to a fool-and-a-half make a bigger fool out of himself, but . . ."

"It's not presumptuous, Bax. And there's nothing foolish about it."

"Well," says Baxter. "I'm glad you feel like that." He looks down at her until she looks up at him.

"I'm really happy you feel like that," he repeats.

"I've felt that way all along, Bax. You just never gave me a chance to say so."

Slowly he leans over and kisses Louise, first on the forehead, then, as she raises her face to him, on the lips. The kiss lasts long enough to be remembered. Then Baxter walks to the door and leaves.

HE MAN WITH THE TROMBONE CASE will watch the boy and his mother pass by him. He will not notice the dog in the crate that the boy is carrying, and the dog's sudden staccato barks will startle him.

The man will turn to the doors leading to the taxi stands and see that the crowd there is slimmer than it has been for some time. He can see two porters near the curb, but there is no policeman. Then the man will face the large window in the terminal where most of the passengers are either seated on the packed benches or watching a newly parked helicopter, its blades rotating slowly to a stop. Keeping the trombone case beside him on the floor, the man will kneel and retie the shoelaces of his right shoe tightly. When he finishes with the right shoe, he will retie the laces of his left shoe. He will be breathing like a runner about to start a race.

At the exact moment when a woman's voice on the loudspeaker will begin announcing in English, Spanish and French that the flight to London will be delayed by one hour, the man will finish tying the shoelaces of his left shoe. Still kneeling, he will slide the trombone case in front of him and open it. He will busy himself with something in the case for a few moments, then remove a barrel-stunted automatic rifle from the case. He will move quickly now, stationing himself directly beneath but slightly in front of the passenger footbridge above him.

At that exact moment the two Franciscan nuns will be watching the helicopter blades stop completely. The boy with the crated dog will be adjusting himself in a small bench opening beside his mother. A Puerto Rican family—a father, a mother and two teenage sons—will be picking up their luggage and heading for their flight gate. One of the boys will notice the man with the rifle under the footbridge, tug at his father's sleeve and say, "Un soldado, Papá. Hay un soldado allá."

"AX," TOM SHOUTS INTO THE TELEPHONE. "You must be crazy. Why in the hell do you want to go back into that cauldron? You've paid your dues there."

"It'll be a brief stint this time," Tom hears Baxter say. "I just want to get a picture or two that I've been looking for. In fact, it all comes down to one picture. As soon as I get it, I'll pack up and leave."

"But don't you know what they think of Americans now in that part of the world? Haven't you been reading the papers? They kidnap any American they can get their hands on. Bax, you're not thinking."

Tom listens for an answer, but there is none. At last, when he is about to break the silence, he hears Baxter say, "I'm calling you from New York right now, Tom. I'm booked on the regular TWA flight to London. Then from London to Cyprus. And from Cyprus I'll find my way by ferry to a port above Beirut. It's done all the time."

"But you're an American, Bax. And on top of that you're an American with a high profile. Americans have a way of disappearing in Lebanon. And once they disappear, they don't surface."

"Well, I'm not exactly a beginner, Tom. I know the ropes. I know the places to avoid. I'll be as careful as I can. I'm not out to be a martyr. I've graduated from that phase."

"You won't let me talk you out of this?"

"Next time, Tom."

"Call me from somewhere over there. The phones still work."

"No promises, but I'll try."

"What do you want me to tell Louise? She's sure to ask."

"Stall her as long as you can. I've already told her I'm going away. I just never told her where. I may be back before she realizes I'm gone."

"I really can't believe this conversation, Bax. I can't believe I'm talking to you like this—"

"Have to go, Tom. Give my love to Linda and the kids. Good-bye."

Tom listens and then stares at the phone as the line goes blank. Then he slams the receiver into its cradle and swings his desk chair around with such force that he almost comes full circle.

"That fool," he says aloud. He is sitting with his back to his desk, so he does not hear Louise enter his office. "That damned fool!"

"Not me, I hope," says Louise.

Startled, Tom wheels his chair around and faces her.

"Not you what?" he asks.

"I hope I'm not the damned fool."

"No, no. How long have you been in the office?"

"I just came in. Just this minute." She pauses and smiles, hoping that Tom will change his mood, but there is no change.

"Well, what's up, Louise?"

"Not much. Just reporting on *Stills in Motion*. I've arranged for it to premiere a week from this Saturday. Eight o'clock. It's a good hour. After the news. I've coordinated with Promotion, and they're working on a brief campaign to publicize it. Actually it won't take much. A lot of people have been waiting for this."

"Good," answers Tom distractedly. "Good, that's all to the good."

Louise waits for him to catch her eyes, but he busies himself with some papers on his desk.

"Anything wrong, Tom?" she asks tentatively.

Tom continues to sort through the papers. Louise has the impression that he is sorting through them a bit too deliberately. When she looks down at them, she sees that they are upside down. She reaches down and turns them right side up for him.

"I think they'll make more sense this way."

Tom brushes them aside.

"Maybe I should leave and come back later," she says and turns to the door. She is almost at the door when she hears Tom say, "He's going back, Louise."

"Who?"

"Bax."

"Back where?"

"Back to Lebanon."

"Back to Lebanon," she says incredulously. "He told me he was going to take a month or two off. I never thought he—"

"I just found out myself. He just called me before you came in. He's at Kennedy right now waiting for a flight to London."

"Tom, you can't be serious."

"I wish I weren't."

"But why is he doing this?"

"Who knows? He said something about getting a picture he didn't get the last time. It's crazy."

"We have to stop him. We have to talk him out of going."

"I tried that when I had him on the phone, Louise. No luck."

"But we have to do something. He just can't go back there again."

"What can we do?"

"I'm going," Louise states.

"Going?"

"I'm going to Kennedy. There's a shuttle. We still have time. Those overseas flights all leave around seven or eight. We have two and a half hours. What airline is he taking?"

"I don't even remember. He called from Kennedy and said he was getting the regular flight to London." He pauses, trying to remember. "TWA. He said he was calling me from the TWA terminal."

"I know that flight. It leaves after dinner. We have more than two and a half hours, Tom. That's time enough if we leave right now." She looks at her watch. "We can get the next shuttle if we rush."

Tom is already putting on his coat.

"Do you need anything, Louise?" he asks.

"Just my purse."

"I'm ready. Get your purse, and let's go."

Together they run out of the office, and Louise grabs her purse from her desk as they pass it.

"He's falling back into the same old pattern, Tom. I thought he'd put it behind him, but he hasn't."

"It's all about a picture he wants to take." He pauses as they continue walking together. "The day you see me risk my life for one picture, Louise, is the day you have my permission to question my sanity."

"Hurry, Tom, please."

16

THE GIRL IS WALKING with her older sister across the footbridge to the cafeteria in the TWA terminal. She stares at a man in a raincoat who is leaning on the railing of the bridge and looking casually at the crowd below. What she is staring at is not the man but the two cameras that are looped from black straps around his neck. When she and her sister are abreast of the man, she stops.

"Come on, Emily," says her sister, tugging her.

Emily frees herself from her sister's grip and tugs at the

man's raincoat. The man turns and faces her and smiles.

"Can I take a picture?" she asks.

Baxter keeps smiling at the girl and then removes the Hasselblad from around his neck.

"Have you ever taken a picture?" he asks.

"No, but my sister has. She has her own camera."

"How old is your sister?" he asks, looking at the sister.

"She's twelve. Her name's Nancy."

"And what's your name?"

"Emily. I'm eight."

"And you want to take your own picture, Emily, is that right?"

"Yes, please."

"All right. Now hold the camera with both hands like this." He helps her position her hands on the camera. "Good, Emily. Now don't let go. All right. Now look through that little window next to your finger. Good. Can you see me?"

"You look different."

"But that's the way the picture will turn out. You just point the camera at something, and you look through the little window, and then you push this button. Can you feel the button?"

"Yes."

"Good. Now what do you want to take a picture of?"

Clutching the camera like a purse, Emily says, "My Mommy and Daddy are sitting down there. Can I take a picture of them?"

"Down where?" asks Baxter.

"There," says Emily, pointing at the seated and standing and pacing crowd near the large rear window.

"Okay," says Baxter. "Just come over here. Now point the camera where they are."

"I am."

Baxter follows the girl's line of vision to the crowd below. He sees two people who could be her parents, and Emily is aiming the camera in their direction.

"Is your finger on the button?"

"Yes."

When he looks down at the crowd again, he sees Louise hurry to the right flank of the crowd and start to move slowly back toward the center, scanning the crowd as she goes. A second later he hears the first shot.

YOU MUST SEE EVERYTHING THAT HAPPENS in this chapter as happening within the span of a few seconds. You must see it as a photographer would see it.

If you are on the ground level of the TWA terminal, you may be one of those seated before the bay window. If you are, you look now and then at the 747 parked in the light drizzle at the ramp just opposite. Or you read a newspaper. Or you watch the flights being changed regularly on the monitor. Or you sleep.

If you are a boy who knows that he must surrender his crated dog within minutes so that it can be housed in the cargo section of the flight he is about to take with his mother, you squeeze the crate tightly against you. You intend to fight the attendants when they come to take the dog away.

If you are Louise, you have just parted with Tom near the ticket counter and you are looking into the crowd, hoping to see Baxter. You are walking slowly. Once you peek around a lifted, spread-open newspaper to see who is reading it. The reader is a Hassidic rabbi, and he looks at you more out of amusement than anger. You keep walking and looking. Two Franciscan nuns observe you as you pass them. They sit there, cowl-to-cowl, saying little but smiling like young girls. It's apparent that they are looking forward to whatever trip it is they are about to take.

If you are Baxter, you are on the footbridge. You are showing a little girl how to operate your Hasselblad. You are standing beside her as she moves toward the footbridge railing and aims the camera through the bridge uprights at the crowd below.

If you are the man who entered the terminal with a trombone case in hand, you have just finished tying the shoelaces of one of your shoes for the second time. Slowly you open the lid of the trombone case and lift out what looks like an automatic rifle with an abbreviated barrel. You stand up, take a step forward and start firing the rifle in spurts, beginning from your left and heading for the center of the crowd and then the far right where Louise, having heard the first shot, is just turning around.

What happens now is one consequential action after another. As soon as the first shot is fired, there is an instantaneous reaction in the crowd before the bay window. There are the usual screams. The father of the Puerto Rican family stands and puts himself in front of his wife and his young sons. One of the Franciscan nuns, having been hit, has toppled backward off her bench. Several men behind have brought their hands to their faces as if they are preparing to ward off blows or fierce winds or slashing rain. They even half-turn their faces away from the man who is shooting at them. One of the bullets has hit one of the panels of the large rear window. It stays intact. By the time the third bullet hits it, it is already plummeting in shards on the floor and the people beneath. Some of the people on the right side of the crowd, having seen in a split second what is happening to their left, are already on the floor, cowering.

Baxter hears the first shot and sees Louise in the crowd at the same moment. He forgets immediately about Emily, who is still holding the Hasselblad and focusing on her parents in the crowd as he taught her to do. Baxter looks straight down and sees the man with the automatic rifle less than ten feet directly under him. Almost by instinct he knows what is happening. He looks at the quailing crowd before him. He sees the panic and terror in their faces. It is exactly as he has imagined it would be. Automatically he goes for his Nikon, unloops the strap from around his neck and lifts it as he leans against the railing. Amid the rifle fire he will hear himself shout only one word, "Louise!"

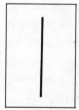

I T WAS THE CAMERA," says Tom. "It must have hit him square. He kept shooting as he fell, but that was just instinct. All the shots went into the ceiling. When the security people took him out of the terminal, he was still unconscious. If you had missed him when you dropped the camera on him, Bax, he would have killed everybody in the place."

Tom, Louise and Baxter are sitting in the lounge of the Ambassador's Club in the TWA terminal. Baxter has just finished being interrogated by the security police. They've returned both of his cameras to him—the Nikon, which is broken in two places and has a trace of blood and human hair on one of its corners, and the Hasselblad, which was retrieved on the footbridge. They've asked him to remain available for a subsequent hearing, but, like Tom, they are convinced that if he had not acted as he did when he did by dropping his camera on the gunman's head the results would have been far worse than they were.

"It's amazing you didn't miss, Bax," Tom says.

"Luck, Tom."

"Thank God."

"Are you all right, Louise?" asks Baxter.

"Well, I'm still shaking. Really, I'm shaking all over. I can't stop it. It's like a nightmare."

Tom stands. "I better call home. Nobody knows I'm here. We left so fast." He heads toward the telephones. The lounge is empty except for several reporters who are still phoning in their stories. The bartender is watching the television screen on which the events of the past hour or so are being flashed.

Louise rises from her chair and sits beside Baxter on the sofa. She acts like a woman who has been exposed to zero temperatures for too long and is unable to get warm. She reaches for Baxter's hand and holds it tightly. He responds by putting his free arm around her.

"Mayhem incorporated," he says.

"It's exactly what you said might happen."

"I was hoping I was wrong."

"Now everybody knows."

"It'll just be another item on the news, Louise. It will last

a little longer than most items, but it will fade like the rest
of them."

"Is that why you wanted to photograph something like
this?"

"Exactly."

Louise looks him in the eyes. "You could have, Bax.
When it all started, you could have."

"I know."

"But you didn't."

"The thought crossed my mind."

"Why didn't you?"

He returns her look. "You."

They sit in silence after that. Finally, Louise's tremblings
cease, but Baxter keeps his arm around her.

"Do you know what's on my mind now, Louise?"

Louise sits erect and looks into his face. "No," she says.

"I'm wondering if I would have done what I did if you
weren't there. I mean I wonder if I would have done something if someone I knew, someone I loved, wasn't in danger."

"I'm sure you would have done the same thing, Bax."

"I hope so, but I don't know, Louise."

"Don't think about it." She knows that he will keep
thinking about it. She sees in his face the same expression
that she saw when he told her that he felt responsible for
the death of his wife.

"Let's go, Bax. As soon as Tom's off the phone, let's go."

"Where?"

"Well, you still aren't going to Lebanon, I hope."

"No," he says, and pauses. "I don't have to go now. It's
here, Louise. Lebanon's right here."

HE VOICE SHE HEARS IS HERS, and yet it is a
voice she has never heard come from within
her before. It is speaking in a language of its
own, a language she has never used and never
knew she knew. It ends in whimpers and then
a quiet hum as if she is trying to stay in tune
with a melody she can almost hear, but it is fading, fading
slowly but fading nonetheless.

"Louise," he whispers.

"Ssh," she answers. "Ssh, Bax." It is her real voice now,

the voice that she has learned to recognize as hers. She does not want to return to it yet, not quite yet.

"Should I—"

"No shoulds, Bax. Just hold me. Just the way you are. Just like I'm holding you." She tightens her arms and legs around him and eases her grip but only slightly. The feeling of the past few minutes is still sweet to her.

"There's a story I read when I was in Beirut," Bax says after a while. "It's only a half a page long. A man and woman are in a room. They're lovers. Outside, the bombs are falling, and there is the steady sound of artillery. Everybody else in their apartment building has fled or is huddling in the basement. But the two lovers stay in their room. They won't let the war dictate the kind of life they should live. Their lovemaking tells the war to go to hell. Life over death. Something like that. They don't scare. And the bombs continue to fall." He pauses and kisses her on each eyebrow, then on the lips, then on her forehead, then on the lips again. When the kiss is over, he lets his cheek slide slowly against hers. "I've always seen that story as a kind of prophecy. It just tells me that we're all at war. Anything can happen. Anything can happen anytime, anywhere. Love's your only weapon, your only shelter."

"I don't hear any bombs, Bax."

"You don't have to hear them. What happened at the airport was something like that. It brought it all home. Beirut happened right in Kennedy Airport, and the only reason we're here is because I dropped a camera on a man with an automatic weapon and was lucky enough to hit him, to bring him down."

Louise turns her face away, remembering the havoc at

the terminal and resenting how the memory of it gradually begins to usurp the joy she feels in the moment. She remembers how they said good-bye to Tom and how the police asked Bax to stay for questions in the morning. They gave him a number to call. She remembers how she just told Tom that she was staying, how she and Bax taxied into Manhattan, how they checked in at the Hotel Pierre and how, once in their room, she could no longer contain the tension of the entire afternoon and evening and gave in to the tears that were waiting to be shed in deep, breath-denying gasps that left her shuddering helplessly long after she had no more tears to give. Bax soothed her then, sat beside her on the bed and held her until the shudders stopped. Then they lay together, she in his arms and he in hers and both still in their streetclothes, until she was warm again and with every passing minute more and more distanced from what happened at the terminal. Later when they lay together under the sheet and single blanket, she did not think of anything more than being as close to Bax as possible, as if they were two survivors of a wreck at sea and had only one another to cling to for their salvation. And then without a word and without any preliminaries at all, she let him into her as if this were just the final consequence of their need, and what she felt after that was so far different from what she had ever felt with Harry that she believed that her life was happening for the first time at that moment, that everything before that had been an enacting of what she thought life was.

"It was all a sham, Bax," she whispers.

"What was?"

"Me. Everything about me."

"You don't have to say that."

"I do. I have to. I have to hear myself say it."

She still holds him within her as they turn on their sides. Her breasts settle slowly against his chest. She had almost stopped thinking of them as breasts. They were for so many months just parts of her that she washed when she showered or slung into the pink cups of a brassiere or, with fear in her fingertips, examined tentatively for lumps or thicknesses. Now they are her true breasts again, and she wants them to shape themselves against Bax's chest. She wants that more than anything else she can think of at that instant. Even when she feels him naturally withdrawing from inside of her, she tightens her legs around him to prevent it from happening. It is not more pleasure she wants. She simply wants his life to remain part of her.

"Bax," she says.

"At your service."

"I'm afraid I'll be hard to get rid of."

"I'm not thinking about it."

"I don't mean that the way it sounds. I'm not talking like a planner. What happened at Kennedy just wiped that away, honest to God. I'm not thinking about the past either. I'm just living right now. And I want to keep living right now as long as right now is there to live. Does that sound crazy?"

"I've been doing it for years, Louise. That means that both of us are crazy."

"I want to be crazy with you. I want to stay crazy with you." She laughs and nuzzles against him.

"It's not as easy as it sounds, dear."

Slowly and carefully he separates himself from her and sits on the edge of the bed. He remains that way for several moments and then leans forward, resting his elbows on his knees.

"Once you're crazy, Louise, you can't go back. Do you know what I mean? You have to go where you think you should be. You can't settle for a loft some place so that you can develop exquisite pictures."

From somewhere in predawn Manhattan she can hear a siren unfurl its scream into space. It goes on without a break in pitch until sheer distance makes it diminuendo into silence again.

"Did you hear that?" he asks.

"The siren?"

"Yes."

"I heard it."

"That's the only clock there is. It doesn't have to be a real siren like that one. It can be a phone call, a news item, a letter, something that comes into your head while you're thinking about something else. But they all have the same purpose."

"Do you think that what happened at the airport was just the beginning, Bax?"

"Maybe. Maybe not. But it happened. And if it can happen once, it can happen again."

"Is there anything we can do?"

"Not much." He turns to her. "I learned in Lebanon, Louise, that there are a lot of people who aren't ready to forgive Uncle Sam. A lot of them have seen people close to them killed with our approval or with our silence, which amounts to the same thing. And they want justice, their kind of justice. It's not just going to fade away. I'm not talking about governments now. I'm talking about individuals. A man from a village. A student. Somebody's sister. Somebody's cousin. Anybody."

"But they have to be a minority."

"It doesn't matter how many. One is enough. One here. One there. It adds up." He looks away from her and stares at the darkness in the corner of the room as if there is something there that only he can see. "You know about those killer ants in Africa, don't you, Louise?"

"I've heard of them."

"Let me tell you how they can kill an elephant. It's not a pretty sight. They know they can't penetrate the hide. So they crawl into his eyes, his nostrils, his anus. Zillions of them. They get to his soft spots. And pretty soon the elephant is so desperate that he goes mad. He can't get rid of them, can't fight them. He can't trample them because they're in him. So he sometimes butts his skull against a tree or a rock because he's gone mad with what the ants are doing to him. And he ends up by killing himself with his own violence." He looks back at her. "It's not a nice picture, but you can draw the parallels yourself."

"It's terrifying."

"It's also possible. That man with the automatic rifle back at Kennedy—you heard what they learned about him from his passport. He was from *that* part of the world. He wasn't some disgruntled employee. Multiply him by God knows how many, and you see a possible future."

"Bax."

"Yes."

"I don't want to hear any more."

"It's an ugly prospect, I know. Maybe I shouldn't have mentioned it, but that's the world I see, the world I live in."

She puts her hand on his back. It calms her just to touch him, to maintain the contact of palm and shoulder blade. Slowly he lies back on the cooling sheet beside her. She puts her arms across his chest and presses her cheek against the muscle of his upper arm. For a moment she imagines that she is the woman in the story Bax read in Beirut. She and Bax are alone in their apartment. There is a duel of artillery in the hills above Beirut. A jet begins its dive and fires the hiss of its missiles at someone else's apartment. She hears the missiles hit and knows that somewhere someone is dying or already dead. She lifts herself up slightly and kisses Bax on the cheek, then slides her kiss across his cheek to his lips. Still kissing him, she folds her leg lightly over his body. She feels his fingers in her hair, and the reaction in the tips of her breasts is a tightening of pleasure that almost hurts her. She hears the siren again, and it is coming closer and closer. By the time it reaches the hotel and passes on, Louise does not even notice it. She is moving against Bax and with him, and she feels such a new and enlivening sense of herself that she thinks she cannot contain it. She knows that each day to come will be totally unlike any other, totally unpredictable and unschedulable, and the only continuity in her life will be a repetition of what she is experiencing this instant. The memory of the lovers in Beirut transforms itself into the fierce clasp that she is both giving and receiving. The roostering siren that is ebbing down some side street is blurring like the dream of her old life that she is already starting to forget.

20

Remember Emily? After Baxter showed her how to point the Hasselblad and how to press the button that would take the picture, she remained poised at the railing even after the shooting started. When she finally did take the picture, panic had already seized the crowd in front of the bay window.

Weeks after the incident at the TWA terminal, Baxter develops the roll of film in the Hasselblad together with some of his other negatives. When he prints Emily's photograph, he is dumbfounded. It is "his" picture, the "ultimate photograph," but he cannot remember how it was taken. Then he recalls the little girl named Emily on the foot-bridge.

The developed photograph shows everyone in the frame in some stage of terror. The Franciscan nun is just starting to topple backward from her bench seat. The Puerto Rican father is just beginning to react. The people nearest the large rear window are crowding together as if their very density might serve as their protection. The bullet holes in the terminal window itself are clearly visible.

Baxter works on various prints, refining and refining and refining until he realizes the best blend of shading and light. The result is as perfect as a photograph can be. He has even cropped the picture so that it seems tilted and slightly off center, and this has the effect of intensifying the chaos in the photograph itself. He considers entitling the picture "A Child's View of the Next War." Then, for reasons that he will never be able to explain to himself or to anyone else, he takes the finished print and the negative, scissors them quickly into smaller and smaller pieces and drops them like a handful of ashes into the wastebasket.